Lord of the Elements

(Book 2 in The Last Observer Series - A prequel)

By

G. Michael Vasey

Note to readers – although this is the prequel to The Last Observer, it is Book 2 in the series and it contains massive spoilers that will make your enjoyment of **The Last Observer** *less – please do read that book before starting this one – thank you!*

Magic is real. It is all around you, but most importantly, it is inside of you.

"One only has to seal a goblet full of compressed Air, Water, or Earth and to leave it exposed to the Sun for a month. Then separate the Elements scientifically, which is particularly easy to do with Water and Earth. It is marvelous what a magnet for attracting Nymphs, Sylphs, and Gnomes, each one of these purified Elements is....."

Compte de Gabalis, Abbe N. de Montfaucon de Villars.

Copyright ©2017 Asteroth's Books
All rights reserved

Text copyright: G. Michael Vasey
ISBN: 978-0-9961972-7-4

All rights reserved. Except for brief quotations in critical articles or reviews, no part of this book may be reproduced in any manner without prior written permission from the publisher.

The rights of Asteroth's Books and author have been asserted in accordance with the Copyright Designs and Patents Act 1988.

Table of Contents

CHAPTER 1 - BORN OF FIRE ... 9
CHAPTER 2 – LATE TO A MEETING ... 12
CHAPTER 3 – OUIJA GAMES ... 21
CHAPTER 4 – PUTTING THINGS RIGHT ... 25
CHAPTER 5 – THE GRAND MASTER ... 28
CHAPTER 6 – A FIND ... 31
CHAPTER 7 – A MEETING IN THE DESERT ... 33
CHAPTER 8 – GRIMOIRE OF EL NETLAZ ... 37
CHAPTER 9 – GOING HOME ... 42
CHAPTER 10 – THE BEAST WITHIN ... 45
CHAPTER 11 – THE PROMISE ... 48
CHAPTER 12 – THE LODGE MEETS ... 59
CHAPTER 13 – BETRAYAL ... 66
CHAPTER 14 – ASTRAL THREAT ... 72
CHAPTER 15 – MEISTER ... 78
CHAPTER 16 – FIND EDWARD ... 82
CHAPTER 17 – A COMMAND ... 85
CHAPTER 18 – THE FIRST BATTLE OF GROSVENOR STREET ... 88
CHAPTER 19: A DECISION IS MADE ... 94
CHAPTER 20 – A RITUAL ATTEMPTED ... 97
CHAPTER 21 – ZELTAN TAKES COMMAND ... 102
EPILOGUE ... 108
OTHER BOOKS FROM ASTEROTH'S BOOKS ... 111
    THOMAS BAUERLE ... 111

G. MICHAEL VASEY 111
SAM WHITE 112

Chapter 1 - Born of Fire

Candlelight flickered and danced dimly against the chiseled and cobwebbed walls of the crypt. Eerie shadows moved lazily in tune to the candle's dancing flame across roughly hewn rock and occasional brickwork. Somewhere deep within the semi-lit gloom, a voice was slowly chanting strange words; its intonation rising and falling hypnotically. A thick and acrid smoke rose from a stone incense burner strategically placed beside the single white candle that rested on top of a block of roughly hewn stone. Pungent incense filled the dark, dank space and hung heavily in the air like an early morning fog. The chanting paused for a moment as the hooded and cloaked figure stood up and drew in a deep and deliberate breath of the incense-charged air.

Raising his arms in the air to the point that they almost touched the uneven ceiling of the crypt, Galivar concentrated, using every ounce of will that he could muster, before finally forcefully intoning the words of power in a deep and rich voice. Orange flames shot up in front of him, forming a sheer wall of brightness and intense heat. Galivar allowed himself just the hint of a smile of triumph.

"All those years of study and work had finally paid off."

He had indeed managed to work a very powerful act of element magic complete with a strong physical manifestation of one of the elements. In this case, Fire. Beads of sweat began to roll down his greying temples as the heat in the crypt became stifling. However, before Galivar could continue with his ritual, all hell broke loose.

"Satan worshipper," someone screamed from behind him.

Three hooded and cloaked men sprung up in unison from the shadows. Dressed in dark habits and bearing iron crucifixes, they rushed at Galivar as one.

"Demon summoner," they shouted.

The crypt exploded in sounds as they leapt upon Galivar, dragging him roughly to the floor where they pummeled him with their fists. As they attacked Galivar, another more sinister sound began to envelope the crypt. It was laughter. A deep and evil laughter that made the blood run cold despite the burning heat. The laughter echoed and boomed inside the cave-like space, building in wave after wave of ear piercing sound. Louder and louder it grew, bouncing from wall-to-wall, and gaining in volume, as if it was amplified and magnified exponentially through time.

The monks' efforts to drag Galivar to the ground and hold him there were thwarted by the sound of this evil, hate-filled, laughter that rose from all around the crypt; growing in volume and intensity until their ear drums were pierced and then, finally exploded. Galivar also heard the laughter. He watched as the wall of flame turned from red and yellow to the color of congealed blood. Within the flames, he and the monks saw just the hint of a face appear. Galivar knew that this interruption by his colleagues had taken place at a key, critical, and most unfortunate point in his bold invocation and, unlike the monks who stared in horror at what they saw before them, he knew that it was already too late.

The monks turned and ran screaming with blood gushing from their eyes and their ears. They rent and tore at their clothes as if, they too, were aflame; while the skin of their faces and hands shriveled and boiled in the heat. One fell, tripping just before making it to the rough stone steps that provided the only exit to the crypt. He lay there writhing and screaming in agony on the floor as his clothes finally burst into flames. His screams of terror and pain simply added to the cacophony of strange sounds now reverberating around the small cavern.

The face in the flame grew larger in size slowly becoming more definite and, just as Galivar felt the face might actually consume him, there was an abrupt and very loud cracking sound and it was gone. The face, the flames, and the terrible sounds were all gone in an instant. Only a hint of acrid smoke was left behind.

Galivar gingerly picked himself up. One side of his face was badly burned and shriveled, and his ears still rang with the sound of that hellish laughter. He surveyed the scene briefly and then he too began to run. He ran just as fast as he could. Out of the crypt, out of the monastery, and out into the open countryside. He ran and ran until he felt he could run no more.

"What have I done?" he asked himself in horror.

There was no going back now. His secure and safe existence as a monk was over. He would be a marked and wanted man sought by the Church he had served to face punishment for sorcery and possibly even worse. He began to trudge through the wet mud of the forest that he found himself in not knowing what he would do or where he would go. Somehow, he would have to make amends and put right the wrong that he had done this morning. Even it took an eternity.

Chapter 2 – Late to a Meeting

Edward was puzzled. Very puzzled. Anyone who took the time to note his furrowed brow and partially closed eyes would know this. He had been listening intently to the lecture. Something the Lecturer had just said had caught and then held his attention. His mind racing to try to find the loopholes or flaws in the argument that he had just heard. In the background, the Lecturer's voice droned on until interrupted by the stark ringing of a bell. Edward jumped, his attention snapping back to the matter at hand.

"Not paying attention, huh, Bright?" said the Lecturer.

Edward flushed slightly as he saw that all eyes in the room were upon him. There was a giggle or two from somewhere towards the back of the classroom.

"No Sir," he lied. "But I do have a question."

"It will have to wait Bright, I'm afraid."

The droning figure was already on his way to the door of the classroom. "I have another appointment to make," he said.

Edward sat back on the hard, but highly polished wooden bench. Many other backsides must have warmed that seat across the years to deliver such a deeply ingrained and perfect polish to the woods' surface. He waited for his classmates to leave in a cacophony of verbal diarrhea, backslappings, and door slamming. Finally, Edward was alone, left to savor the inevitable silence of the now empty classroom. Something he had just learned had struck a chord with him and now many thoughts ricocheted around his mind knocking various other ideas out in the process; creating a stream of interconnected thoughts that now echoed and jostled each other through the workings of his brain.

The math teacher had made a rather simple observation, he recalled. He had remarked that the hexagram as a shape, displayed perfect symmetry around a single point. The chain of thoughts that had followed included a consideration of the concept of 'as above, so below' as well as the four elements. The four elements are symbolized by both the hexagram symbol itself with its intersecting triangles of Fire, Water, Earth, and Air, and by the equal-armed cross that can be drawn through the hexagram. Edward's thoughts had simply exploded at that point; darting off in many different directions and he was now struggling to collect all of the strands back together succinctly so that he could make sense of it. He needed to write this all down and instinctively he reached for a piece of off-white paper that still lay in front of him and began to scribble on it furiously. His mind was still on fire as his hand moved across the page naturally lagging behind his thoughts and leaving an almost undecipherable scrawl behind it.

Edward had become interested in all matters esoteric at a relatively early age. He had read avidly anything remotely labelled as 'occult' that he could lay his hands on, but the vast majority of such material in those days was about séances, ghosts, and such. It was largely spiritualism. Very frustrating and 'quite a lot of Victorian drivel' was how he had come to think about it.

Somewhere in his late teens, Edward had taken up meditation while his friends had taken up girls, and he would happily spend his free time sat bolt upright with his eyes closed, actively exploring his inner worlds. His interest in arcane symbols had led him naturally to an interest in mathematics. Mathematics was the language of God. It was neat. It was succinct. It had God's name written all over it. Furthermore, he had developed a strong interest in numbers, their esoteric meaning, and how to look at the numerical value of words to draw connections between them.

Edward still wrote furiously at his desk. How to capture all of these divergent thoughts in his notes? This was where a mathematical formula might come in handy if it were possible, as it could almost certainly describe the model behind his thinking and encompass the grand design.

"Edward."

This time, he heard the voice and he peered in the direction of the doorway, screwing his face up in a vain attempt to overcome his natural shortsightedness.

"Edward," said the voice, louder, and more insistently this time.

"Yes?" Edward replied, though not entirely too sure to whom.

"Edward, it's time," exclaimed the disembodied voice.

"Time," thought Edward.

"Edward. Let's go before we are too late.

"Oh, bloody hell," said Edward inadvertently, as he recalled that he did have a rather important appointment. In one move, he scooped up his papers, pens, pencils and rulers sweeping them into his briefcase and running down the steps of the lecture hall towards the door.

"Yes, Sorry Tony, I completely forgot"

The look on Tony's face showed no surprise.

"Absent-minded as usual," said Tony. "Come on, we are already going to be late and you know he doesn't like us to be late."

Edward knew that Tony was right. This little monthly meeting for those interested in strange and esoteric phenomena was both organized and managed by one Dr. Ambrose Pringle. Dr. Pringle was 'old school'. He expected refined manners from his students and that certainly included the courtesy of being prompt and on time.

"Let's get our skates on then Tony," said Edward.

It wasn't so far to go. It was a meeting room off campus about a quarter of a mile away in Dr. Pringle's favorite pub. The pub was supposed to be haunted by the ghost of a student who had failed his examinations and on the point of ruination over his gambling bills, had hung himself from the beams in a room upstairs over the bar. Edward suspected this to be hogwash. He thought it highly likely that it was simply a good marketing strategy and a great story on the part of a bold proprietor.

As they hurried down the already darkening lane between the library building and the science department, it began to rain.

"Bugger," exclaimed Tony. "I didn't bring a coat."

Neither had Edward. Edward was dressed in his usual grey suit with blue tie. His fellow students often laughed at his appearance and nicknamed him the 'businessman', but Edward had neither the time nor the inclination to spend time looking at clothes. A suit was always easy to find. The shirts easy to wear and the tie was a going away gift from his Auntie. Suits were simply entirely practical unless one was about to engage in some heavy labor, which, of course, Edward always carefully avoided.

The rain began to pick up steam. It now pounded the pavement and a smell of dampness rose from the dry concrete and thirsty grass. At this rate though, that aroma wouldn't last long as the volume of water now falling would drown it out, and the two boys would arrive totally and utterly drenched.

"Quick, in here," shouted Tony, pushing Edward into a doorway.

"But we'll be late!"

"That's OK. Now we have an excuse," Tony pointed out.

"It's not that much further," said Edward. "We can make a run for it?"

Tony peered out into the growing darkness and the wall of water in front of them and then down at himself. "I'm drenched already and I don't fancy getting any wetter thank you,"

Edward had to agree that this was not actually a practical idea. He leaned back against the door and it gave suddenly, opening wide, so that Edward stumbled backwards and through the doorway into the darkness.

"Where are you going?" laughed Tony, in mock surprise.

Edward managed to stop himself from falling completely over and found himself in a hallway that led several feet to another door. It was some sort of porch it seemed and there, in the corner, was a brolly, propped up by the door. Edward picked it up, opened it, and with a look of triumph on his face, shouted "Come on. Let's make that dash for it now."

Tony and Edward raced down the street and around the corner. The brolly kept the worst of the rain off them both until they reached the tiny pub.

"I'll just return it tomorrow," said Edward.

Tony nodded. "That was a stroke of luck!" he said.

The Dog and Duck was more like a hole in the wall than a proper pub. It consisted of a pokey bar that realistically only had room for four adults at a crush and a small room next door that was laughingly called a Lounge. The Lounge contained just two tables and eight chairs. The pub didn't do brisk business in the winter simply because it was so tiny, but whenever the sun shone and the weather was warm enough, it thrived by virtue of the very large courtyard it could muster and a super student-priced menu that appealed to all in the vicinity of the University.

The bar was dimly lit and quite smoke-stained, so that it was difficult to see even in such a miniature place. It stank of stale beer and cigarettes, making it somewhat unpleasant to the olfactory sense. The door to the Lounge had a piece of paper stuck to it with sticky tape that simply read – Reserved.

Edward pushed open the door and walked in.

"Ah, Finally," said a rather refined voice. "I was rather afraid our little get together would be a total washout this evening."

Edward was quite surprised to see just three other people in the Lounge. Dr. Pringle, immediately noticeable because of his unkempt wiry silver hair and ruddy complexion, sat in the corner and to either side of him were the 'ladies'. The ladies smiled up at them as they entered, peering through their small spectacles as if inspecting something quite suspicious and perhaps not very wholesome.

"Come on in then," said Pringle rather impatiently.

Edward took the seat nearest to the door after shaking the wet brolly briskly and placing it, folded carefully, by the door. Tony sat down beside him.

"Apologies Dr. Pringle. The rain." said Tony in explanation nodding his head towards the small window. "It's pelting down."

"Yes, my dear boy, the rain."

There was a moment's silence before Pringle peered around

his audience and began again.

"Well, perhaps we should begin. On a night like tonight, one can hardly expect a full house, can one?"

The 'ladies' nodded in unison like two nodding headed dogs of the type that one might find on the dashboard of a car.

"Tonight, I had thought to discuss the topic of psychism," began Pringle pushing his glasses up his short-upturned nose.

Some might argue that Dr. Pringle lacked a true nose having instead, two small holes above his upper lip that passed for nostrils. His lack of a true nasal appendage made it difficult for him to wear glasses and he had to keep pushing them onto his face as a result. His brown eyes were deeply set and appeared extraordinarily large behind said glasses. His furry grey eyebrows, mass of untidy hair, and an angular chin, meant that Dr. Pringle was actually quite an unforgettable sight.

"However, with so few in attendance, perhaps we should simply open up for discussion and save my considered views on that topic for a better attended session?"

The ladies nodded furiously.

"Good, well, where shall we begin?" said Pringle expectantly looking around the room.

"Have you ever met a real magician?" asked Tony almost immediately. "You know, someone that could really make physical magic?"

Pringle peered across the table at Tony his eyes seeming even larger and very brown through the glasses. "Oh yes, my dear boy, I have,"

Edward was surprised. In all past meetings, Pringle had never mentioned meeting any magician, but had rather lectured on about topics such as his favorite psychism topic and other areas like the nature of the astral plane and its occupants. He had never before referenced magic, but stayed with more theosophical subjects and content.

"Really?" said Edward.

"Indeed yes," affirmed Pringle. "It was a strange meeting and

I have subsequently doubted that it ever really occurred in this reality, but it did and I have never quite seen things the same way since," said Pringle.

Edwards's interest was piqued and he leaned in closer towards Dr. Pringle, as did the others.

"It was many years ago. I had just graduated myself and was working on my Doctorate," began Pringle visibly pleased with the sudden interest around the table. "One evening, I had gone out for a stroll around Soho. There were lots of old shops selling curiosities there back then and I found one in particular that seemed intriguing. It was very small and could hardly have done much business, but it sold books mainly. I stepped in to browse. Most of the books were original editions and apparently quite rare, so maybe that was how the place survived, I don't really know. Anyway, as I was browsing, I became aware of two gentlemen having a conversation behind me." Pringle took a small sip of his half pint of beer noting that he still had the room's entire attention. "Of course, I couldn't help but listen in."

"Yes," said Edward.

Dr. Pringle peered down into his glass of beer and rolled the remaining contents around the bottom of the glass. "They were talking about a secret occult lodge that apparently met somewhere in the vicinity."

"Really," said Tony in a low murmur.

"Funny really," muttered Dr. Pringle as if to himself. "They caught on to the fact that I was listening after just a minute or so and looked quite alarmed by the fact too I must say. I didn't let on at all and pretended not to have heard a thing browsing through the books."

"Yes, but what did you hear," asked Edward trying to hide his growing excitement.

"Something about elemental magic and a 'Lord'," said Dr. Pringle, now speaking to the group again. "Not enough to learn anything specific, but enough to pique my curiosity. I followed one of them of course."

You could have heard a pin drop as the ladies, Tony, and Edward all waited for Dr. Pringle to continue with his story.

"That's where it all gets very strange and it's why I have been interested academically in the subject ever since. I picked the smaller of the two men and I followed him at a distance. I didn't know it then, but looking back, he must have known that I was following him all along. It was only a short distance before he turned and stared directly at me. That look! I cannot ever forget it. He commanded me with words that spoke to me in my mind asking me to explain myself. I told him, of course, in my thoughts, that I was curious. He asked me what I had overheard. Imagine, not a single word passed our lips at all as I answered him involuntarily in my thoughts and he laughed, laughed at me, out loud." Pringle's voice had trailed off as his memory of that night took over. The look on his face was one of puzzlement and wonder like a small boy. "How did we communicate like that, I wonder?" he said finally.

There was silence. The ladies began to fidget uncomfortably.

"How indeed," said Edward in a low voice, "And what then?"

Dr. Pringle looked up and into Edward's face. The look on his face was one that suggested he was trying to be honest in a crowd that plainly thought him insane. "He told me to go and never come back." he said finally and then looked down at the table almost in shame. "I was so utterly afraid, so personally invaded by darkness, so scared, that I did exactly as he told me."

Edward thought Dr. Pringle was about to cry. He looked distraught just reliving the experience. The ladies looked slightly concerned for him and made cooing noises under their breaths.

"Where was this, do you recall?" asked Edward.

"Somewhere down on Grosvenor Lane as I remember, but I'm not really that sure now. You understand that to me, as a scientist, what happened that day was and still is, absolutely impossible. Unexplainable. Don't you dare tell anyone that I told you this." asserted Pringle suddenly. "They will think me mad, quite mad. Some suspect as much already."

"You have our word," said Tony. Edward nodded. The ladies did too.

Chapter 3 – Ouija Games

The Ouija board had seen much better days and the makeshift wine glass that the four of them now touched with their fingers, would have difficulty moving over the deeply cracked and wrinkled surface of the board. Janet had found it in an old cardboard box in the attic and while its provenance could not be readily ascertained, it must surely have once belonged to a student who had also occupied number 61 Drake Lane. Luckily, there were five wine glasses in the house, the sixth, which made up the original set, had been dropped at some time in the past. Four of the glasses had seen some heavy usage during the course of the evening as the friends consumed three bottles of cheap Spanish wine. As the wine had begun to run out, their spirits had increased under the influence of the bubbly cheap alcohol and that was when Janet suddenly remembered the old Ouija board. The four of them now sat hunched around the kitchen table, fingers on the remaining upturned glass, giggling.

"Nothing's going to happen,'" said Billy, who out of the four, was still the soberest.

"Give it a try Billy," said Janet, rolling her eyes. "Just give it a try..."

The four settled down again looking intently at the upturned glass in silence. It was at that moment that the back door cracked as the latch was turned and opened. Edward caught a glimpse of the four of them jumping in unison as their fearful expectation of something the Ouija board might do turned into group shock as the door opened.

"Bloody hell," shouted Dennis. "You scared the living daylights out of me."

"Good God, my heart is pounding," screamed Janet, between howls of relieved laughter.

Edward surveyed the scene and immediately determined that this activity was not for him. He muttered an apology and made his way through the petite kitchen to the door of the equally miniscule lounge.

"Oh, come on Edward!" said Billy. "Come and join us?"

"Yes...." they all said more or less together. "Do," repeated Janet.

Edward shook his head. "No, I'm sorry. That's playing with fire that is. Nope. Enjoy yourselves, but I am not interested." he said firmly.

"Awwww Edward," moaned Janet. "Always so, ...so boring."

Edward said nothing, but opened the door to the lounge anyway.

"Edward old boy, do you have anything that we can drink?" asked Billy holding out his empty wine glass.

"That I can help with," nodded Edward. "I have a bottle of wine left over from Christmas. I shall go and get it."

He set off decisively, as if to make amends for his lack of interest in the night's activities. He was back less than five minutes later, brandishing a dark bottle that he held aloft to their multiple cheers. He gave it to Billy with a flourish.

"Thanks Edward."

Edward looked a tad embarrassed and was quite relieved to escape the kitchen for the safety of the lounge. He had an interesting book there awaiting him and he would read for a while before going up to bed.

In the kitchen, the new bottle was quickly opened and its contents poured into the waiting and empty glasses.

"To Edward," said Billy before downing a huge gulp of red wine.

"Edward," came back the chorus.

"Do you think it would help if we dimmed the lights a bit?" asked Dennis.

"Why not?" said Billy.

No one objected and so they switched off the lights. It took a while for eyes to accustom themselves to the darkness and refocus on the upturned glass.

Time passed. A heavy silence began to hang over the assembled company in the darkness of the kitchen only interrupted by the now incredibly loud ticking of the ugly, cheap clock that hung over the doorway to the lounge.

"Is there anybody there?" said Janet after several minutes of total silence.

Dennis let out a snigger.

"Sorry, it just sounds so ridiculous," he said.

"Is there anybody there?" repeated Janet, ignoring Dennis.

"Bugger, did you feel that?" asked Billy, as the glass suddenly seemed to lurch sideways.

The glass had seemingly moved abruptly from left to right. It had actually skipped over the deep fold and crack in the old board as if hovering a few millimeters above its' surface.

"Shhhhh," said Janet excitedly.

"Come on, stop pushing the bloody thing," said a skeptical Dennis.

"I'm not," said Janet.

"Me neither," said Billy.

"Nor me," said Guy.

For a moment, the glass was still. Then, slowly and with definite purpose, it began to move again.

"Oh my God," said Guy. "It is moving."

"Problem is we can't see where it is moving to," said Janet.

Suddenly, there was a flash of light as Billy flipped his lighter with his spare hand and held it over the table.

"Good idea," exclaimed Guy.

"Is there anybody here?" asked Janet once more.

The glass moved abruptly and effortlessly across the board settling on top of the letters that spelled 'YES'.

"Oh my God," exclaimed Janet. What is your name?"

The glass moved again. It slipped across the board with ease despite the broken surface.

"F, I, R, E – Fire?" asked Janet in a low husky voice.

The glass began to move again.

"A, I, R – Air?" said Janet tracking the glasses progress.

"Who is pushing it?" asked Billy.

"No one," said Dennis. "It is floating above the board. How is THAT possible?"

"Come on, someone is pushing it."

"Shhhhh," said Janet. "Who is this?"

The glass moved with increased energy.

"L, O, R, D – Lord?" said Janet. "Lord who?"

With that, the glass somehow hurled itself across the room, smashing on the wall above the kitchen sink. Four people screamed involuntarily in unison.

Edward, who was engrossed in his book, only heard muffled screams. Puzzled, he put it down and walked towards the kitchen door. Opening it, he found the room in darkness. He switched on the light. It wasn't so much the four pale and shocked faces peering back at him that attracted his attention as the stacked empty wine glasses perilously sitting atop one another on top of the wine bottle in the middle of the table. Just the slight breeze from pushing open the door was sufficient to send the whole lot crashing to the table in an explosion of broken glass.

"Good God," said Janet. "How did that happen?"

"There, that should teach the lot of you for playing with fire," said Edward.

Chapter 4 – Putting Things Right

Edward started to clean up the glass shards from around the kitchen floor with a little brush and shovel he got from the cupboard under the sink. Four pale and shocked faces watched as he did so. Janet was shaking.

"I did warn you," said Edward gently.

"What exactly happened?" asked Guy incredulously.

"The glass just launched itself at the wall over there," said Janet in a faraway voice. "I wouldn't believe it unless I had experienced it for myself."

"What occurred before that?" asked Edward.

The four told him that they had made contact with an entity. That it had spelt out Fire and Air and the word Lord before the glass had flown across the room and somehow the other glasses had stacked themselves up on top of the board. There was an element of disbelief even as they told their story.

Edward continued to clean up as they related this. "You should all go to bed," he said, as he brushed up more glass shards. He was hoping they would all go quite quickly because he could already sense that something in the room, some presence, needed to be banished and he couldn't perform a banishing ritual with the four of them watching him. They just wouldn't understand, but furthermore, it would scare them even more he felt, and fear was exactly what this type of presence fed on in his experience.

"Come on, the lot of you, off to bed," he commanded.

"I will," said Janet. "I will, but I will sleep with the lights on!"

The three boys also began a movement towards the door.

"Goodnight everyone," said Edward as cheerfully as he could.

After he had cleared the glass and mopped up the remains of the wine, Edward sat in one of the chairs. He straightened his back and closed his eyes, placing both hands on his knees so that he looked rather like a Pharaoh sitting on a throne. He concentrated on clearing his mind, focusing on his breath and breathing in order to do so. He could sense a sort of heaviness around him in the kitchen and there was a just a faint bad smell like rotting drains. Whatever the energy or presence was, it was building, he felt. He focused harder on nothing. He shivered a little, feeling a coldness descending upon him as the rotting drains stench intensified.

"Edward......" hissed a voice in his ear.

Edward jumped, cursed a bit and tried to resettle himself. He hadn't anticipated the voice contact and it had caught him off guard.

"Ha, ha, ha, ha," laughed the same gravelly voice quietly. "Edward."

Edward tried to ignore it and focus again on nothingness. He then stood up abruptly and made three steps forward. He imagined a shaft of the most brilliant white light descending from above him intoning and vibrating a word as he did so. He imagined that light passing through his body and into the floor and as he pictured that in his imagination, he intoned another word. He then imagined a ray of brilliant white light coming from his right and passing through him to the left. Again, he intoned two words as he imagined and visualized this crossing ray of brilliant light.

"Edward, really?" hissed the same voice, still laughing gently.

Edward reached out in front of him and in thin air, drew a pentagram of imaginary light intoning a name. He then carefully moved around ninety degrees and repeated the drawing of a pentagram of light. He did this twice more, turning himself a full 360 degrees to finish where he had started. He then placed his arms out wide speaking intently in a commanding tone of voice before pulling his hands together as if in prayer.

The voice was much fainter as it said, "Edward, you will serve me very well when the time comes."

As Edward repeated the Qabbalistic cross ritual that he had started with, he could feel the kitchen atmosphere returning slowly back to normal. The presence and the hissing voice had both gone, as indeed they must, after the proper performance of the banishing ritual.

Edward sat once more, maintaining his composure for a short while longer, before opening his eyes and mopping his brow with a handkerchief that he had pulled from his pocket. Hopefully, all was well and whatever had been brought through by the séance was now back where it belonged. He was pleased because the entity had been far more powerful than he had at first thought. The voice had been a shock and had momentarily put him off the banishing ritual. He hadn't liked the parting statement much either, but he simply dismissed it as an idle threat given by a mischievous entity.

Chapter 5 – The Grand Master

After his graduation, some six-months later, Edward found gainful employment with relative ease at a private bank. The bank was rather an old-fashioned institution comprised of mostly older male employees who all seemed to wear a standard obligatory uniform of dark suits, white shirts, and blue ties. Edward fit right in. The offices the bank occupied reflected its older world, more traditional, and conservative brand, with its oak paneled rooms complete with large solid oak desks, black telephones, and rather uncomfortable upright seating.

He was offered the position by the Grand Master of a magic lodge that he had joined in his final year at college, taking up an invitation from Dr. Pringle to do so. Apparently, Edward's calm nature and stoic manner had impressed, along with his attitude towards his esoteric studies at the lodge. The Grand Master doubled as the Chairman of the private bank and the bank profited nicely from his position, attracting a steady stream of wealthy individuals recommended by other members of the lodge. Wealth management was something that the bank performed quite well.

Cyril Bainbridge, the Chairman of the bank and Grand Master of the lodge, was in his early sixties. A life behind a sturdy oak desk punctuated by lavish lunches with clients and friends had led to him being of a rather portly disposition. Despite that, Bainbridge seemed a fit and vigorous man who was full of energy and interest in the world. Unmarried, he had only two real passions – bank business and the lodge. In Edward, he had spotted someone whom he felt had similar interests and enthusiasms. It had been the right thing for him to take Edward under his wing to groom him both materialistically and spiritually.

Bainbridge ran private teaching sessions for certain of his lodge members and had almost immediately included Edward in these. In these classes, they studied a variety of topics in greater depth, including qabbalah, astrology, and hermetics. To Bainbridge's delight, Edward lapped up the material and had rapidly become one of the most proactive members both of the group and the Lodge generally. He was, Bainbridge felt certain, his natural successor.

Edward, for his part, quietly enjoyed the tutorship of Bainbridge and began to see him as something of a father figure. Edward's own father had died suddenly when he was just a small child and his mother had never remarried. In fact, he had little or no memory of his father. There was just a vague figure in his memory and a voice that sometimes echoed in his mind that he thought was most likely a recollection of his father's voice. He was, he was told by those who had met his father, his father's double and this seemed to make his mother rather uncomfortable. It was something of a strained relationship with her as a result and Edward had grown self-reliant because of it. He had to be. He had no siblings, little connection to his broader family and a strained relationship with his mother. It was therefore quite natural and somewhat reassuring to have the presence of Bainbridge in his life. However, Edward always had been and always would be a loner. He had little need for company and was quite satisfied with his own. It wasn't friendship that Edward sought from Bainbridge so much as mentorship. He needed someone in his life that could verify his decisions and the general direction that he was taking with life.

Edward may have been a loner, but he wasn't lonely. He led a very active life, both in terms of cultivating his business relationships and in pursuing his love of magic. His small, but neat and ordered apartment comprised simply a living/sleeping room, a small kitchen and a workspace for magic. Here Edward kept his book collection; the most important of which were his own meditation diaries that occupied the entire top shelf of his bookcase each neatly labeled with the time-periods that they covered. The room also contained a variety of rather strange objects. There was a darkened mirror such that the reflection was only dimly visible, a carved wooden box that contained his tarot cards, an ornate silver dagger in an equally ornate sheath, an equal-armed cross made of silver, various other symbols, Egyptian figurines, what appeared to be home-made necklaces of strung beads of different sizes and multiple incense burners. Here, Edward spent much of his free time engaged in meditation, solo ritual, or reading. Indeed, it was where he was sat quietly reading on that day.

The phone in the hallway rang sharply bringing Edward back to reality. He put his book down on the floor besides the old leather armchair that, besides the bookcase and a makeshift altar, was the only furniture in the room. Making his way down the hall, Edward picked up the phone.

"Bright speaking," he said.

"Ah Edward, my dear boy," said the familiar rich tones of Bainbridge. "Can you pop over? I have something I would very much like to show you."

Edward glanced at his watch. "Yes, I can be there in about an hour," he replied replacing the phone back in its holder. He reached for his coat and set off, determined to walk to Bainbridge's for the exercise.

Chapter 6 – A Find

Bainbridge was just a little impatient and as he waited, he allowed himself a whiskey that he took small sips from, savoring the heat and aromatics of the Irish malt. The book lay on his desk in the study. It had a battered and well-used black leather cover, and the inside was full of scribbled notes in a very small hand. Bainbridge flicked through it once more, inspecting one note in particular with a small magnifying glass when he heard the knock at the door. He allowed himself a small smile. He knew that Edward would be excited when he saw this and he could already picture Edward's facial expression in his mind as he examined the book.

The door opened as McMaster showed Edward in to his study.

"Edward dear boy, do come in," he said. "Take a seat and make yourself comfortable. Whiskey?"

Edward declined. "What is it? You sounded excited," he said.

Bainbridge stood up from his chair holding the small battered book and walked around his large oak desk. He seated himself with gravitas in the leather armchair opposite Edward and offered the book to Edward. Edward took it and Bainbridge smiled inwardly as he recognized the look that he had imagined actually pass over Edwards' face. There was a moment of silence as Edward examined the book and then Edward looked up.

"You found it. It exists?"

"Yes, it exists." Bainbridge said.

Edward opened the book once more and flipped through several pages examining both the text and the associated penciled notes.

"Unbelievable," he whispered. "But where...?"

"Baker discovered it. Would you believe in a secondhand store?"

Edward whistled quietly still examining the book.

"Incredible."

"Isn't it indeed," said Bainbridge.

Chapter 7 – A Meeting in the Desert

The sun was dipping slowly behind the horizon, spreading a strange reddened light and very long shadows. The heat of the day was fading fast now that the Sun had more or less set and the chill had made William put up his suit collar. He was cold. The Arizona desert was cold. William mused over the polarity that he saw in the 100+F daytime temperatures and the chilly evening he was now beginning to experience. The last vestiges of sunlight fading, it was already very, very dark as low patchy clouds obscured the stars and the Moon was nowhere to be seen. Reaching into the back seat of the small Ford he had rented, he felt for the blanket that he knew was there. Once he had managed to find it, he spread it around his shoulders as he sat waiting in the darkness. He had little idea of what to expect or indeed, what it was he was actually looking for; he felt a little knot of tightness between his shoulder blades that he recognized as tension and maybe just a little fear.

As the time ticked by – he had no idea how long he had sat there out in the desert – he began to feel sleepy; this despite the fact that his feet felt like two blocks of ice. He must stay awake, observant. He stretched his legs into the pedal area under the dashboard but this only resulted in a very painful cramp in his foot. It was so painful that he had to move quickly, jumping out of the car and walking gingerly up and down for a while. That was when he noticed it. Off in the distance, he saw a flicker of firelight – just briefly and then it was gone again.

Grabbing his flashlight from the passenger seat, William set off as fast as he could towards the location of that momentary flicker of light. This may be the sign he was looking for and it had been no more than 100 yards away he had thought. He had to be careful. The desert was rocky and rough to walk on especially in the dark even with the flashlight whose light covered a small arc around him that seemed to draw the ground up towards him in an optical illusion.

After a short while, he stopped, covered the light and watched and waited, his eyes once again becoming slowly acclimatized to the darkness. His vigilance was soon rewarded with another flicker of light slightly off to his left. Once more, he set off briskly towards it.

William could hear his own breathing. He was beginning to pant due to a combination of the sudden physical exertion and the coldness of the desert air. He was aware that to the one he was seeking, he would resemble some noisy, clumsy city dweller that was rudely upsetting the natural quiet of the desert. He cursed under his breath as he stubbed his toes against a rock and almost tripped so that he fell into his next step jarring his knee painfully in the process. A hand reached out for his arm as he fell forward. The grip was strong and very tight.

"What do you want?" said a voice in the darkness.

"Help," said William. "I need your help."

The grip relaxed and a face appeared out of the darkness just in front of William. Jet-black hair, tanned, and brown eyes. About the only things really visible were the whites of his eyes. It made for an eerie sight.

"Help?" Said the voice.

"Yes. I need help with something that I am told you can help me with." Said William.

"Follow me." Said the voice.

William caught a flash of the man's back in the beam of his flashlight and began to follow as best he could. The man walked fast. Actually, he seemed to simply glide, never bothered by the roughness of the terrain.

"Here," said the voice.

William saw the orange glow of an ember campfire and the man he had sought sitting on a rock by the fire.

"Sit." Commanded the voice.

William sat on a rock and switched off the flashlight waiting a few moments for his eyes to become accustomed to the gloom. The small wiry figure sat opposite him, legs crossed.

"Well?" said the man.

William considered where to begin.

"I am told that you can help me. If what I am told about you is correct, then my story needs no embellishment and I will simply tell you the facts as they stand and hope that you do understand," said William.

The figure nodded.

"I am beginning to question my sanity," said William. "Just two weeks ago everything in my life was boringly very normal. That is, until I was invited to a social event by a very good friend of mine. She told me it would be fun and potentially, very profitable. The party was amazing. There were so many people there that I knew, but only from afar. Politicians, movie stars, models, successful businessmen... I couldn't quite believe my luck."

William shuffled a little trying to find a more comfortable spot on the rock.

"Of all the people that I met there that I could have talked to, it had to be him." He said. Meanwhile, the impassive figure sat motionless across on the other side of the embers.

"He introduced himself as Ralph. He said he wanted to make me an offer. I thought it was going to be some kind of business offer,"

William chuckled to himself.

"His eyes. They were like... the bottomless pit of hell!"

William involuntarily pictured those eyes drawing him in deeper and deeper. He shook and struggled to escape from their icy gaze even in his imagination. "Pits of hell," he repeated as if talking to himself and going silent for a short while.

Suddenly William looked up and across the fire to the other figure. "Oh my God! What have I done?"

"My son, be at peace and continue with your story," said the figure calmly.

William lifted his head from his hands and began again. "He promised me things.... Power, influence, women, money, anything, everything... His eyes! It seemed so reasonable. I knew he could give me whatever I desired. I seemed to have no self, no will. I felt good, powerful, and needy.... Don't you see?" he shouted.

The desert echoed his words back to him..." Don't you see, see, see, see..."

Chapter 8 – Grimoire of El Netlaz

Edward felt a sense of rising excitement as he read. This was it. This was the book he had been searching for. The writer of this book had been a Mage of the first order. In fact, some believed that the writer had actually never really died, but had faked his own death and simply moved on, living an eternal life as a teacher in the shadows. Others claimed that they had met him, or that he still taught them in their dreams. Edward didn't believe anyone who was an adept would truly desire eternal life. More likely, he could simply choose his own time of transition and for now, if he still walked the Earth, he did so with some purpose in mind.

For normal, rational people, these would appear to be the thoughts of a mad man or at least someone with a very strong and perhaps over developed imagination. However, Edward knew of a number of initiates who were reputed to have moved from life to life, staying in the shadows until needed. There was every reason to suspect that the writer of this book was a very high initiate indeed.

The book was really rather cryptic. It read oddly, as if written in some form of code and Edward knew that it was. It wasn't code in the sense that there was some alphanumeric key to decipher the true words, but code in the sense that it was full of symbols whose meaning needed to be unlocked in order to give the whole text meaning. It was an alchemical text and hermetic too. The symbolism was both rich and clever. Devious even. Some of it was beyond Edward. But he knew enough to realize that the book discussed the magical control of the Elements.

In occult circles, the book was only rumored to exist. In their search for it, they had heard many stories, tales, and myths about its origins, existence and, more importantly, the effect that it had had on those who tried to decipher its secret meanings. In those circles, it was known as the Grimoire of El Natlez, or Liber El Natlez.

Its' author was reputed to have been one Brother Galivar of

Bruges. Galivar had lived something of a dangerous double life and consequently was the subject of some very strange and lurid tales. Leading an apparently simple monastic life in the city of his birth, Bruges in Belgium, he had managed to hide his decades of the study of magic. It was said that he had been tutored by none other than the 'real' writer of the works of Shakespeare himself.

Galivar's simple and humble life as a monk had fooled most of those around him. Indeed, he had lived in dangerous times and if anyone had suspected him of his occult double life, his life would have been in danger and he would have faced certain persecution and a horrible death.

The story, while somewhat vague, spoke of a midnight ritual that he had attempted. It had gone badly wrong and caused chaos at his monastery. It had left several monks dead, the Abbott himself injured, and Galivar on the run. No one knew for sure what had happened exactly, but the monks who died were reputedly found in various states of rigor; their faces frozen in masks of horror and badly burned. Rumors were rife of course. Galivar had summoned the very Devil himself, it was said, and he had also been marked by the Devil in a battle of wits and will in the monastery chapel or crypt. The stories said that Galivar's face was frozen down the left side so that it sagged and was useless. A reminder of his arrogance, they said.

The problem with the story was that it had probably been embellished by both his enemies and the Church. Galivar had been painted as a Satanist and sorcerer by the Church of course. Edward and his colleagues at the Lodge however interpreted things very differently. It was not the Devil he had tried to summon but some spirit or entity that he felt it necessary to invoke in order to learn from it.

Galivar was said to have wandered around the continent for years before finally escaping to protestant England where, for a while, he was able to hide himself in the Yorkshire Dales protected by his mentor and moving from place to place. His useless half face though kept loose tongues wagging and rumors of his whereabouts and practices circled and grew. It was said that Beelzebub followed him wherever he went, bringing bad luck, fear and strange events along with him.

How much of this was truth Edward didn't nor couldn't know, but he suspected that much of this part of the story was also embellishment provided by the fears, suspicions, and character of the times. What he did know is that it was during this time of movement and hiding that Galivar wrote his book and having written it, he then simply disappeared and was presumed to have finally died. 'The Devil took his own' was the general consensus at the time. However, that was by no means the end of the story as about 25-years after Galivar's disappearance and supposed demise, he had been possibly recognized as the equally mysterious occult figure known as John of Hedon. Apparently, Galivar had had a small number of students and one of them had accidentally met this John of Hedon at a Sunday market. John of Hedon was a reclusive local landowner in the Yorkshire area who rarely showed his face and, on the occasions that his face was seen, it was said to be greatly dis-figured. John also had garnered a reputation for fortune telling, raising the dead, and several other dubious supernatural activities.

Although John had died and was already buried by the time that Galivar's student made the public statement that John was in fact, Galivar, exhumation of the coffin showed it to be empty except for some large limestone rocks to give it weight. The strange story of Galivar/John did not end there either, as there were those who suggested that Galivar still lived, showing himself only rarely to those who he decided to help. Some said that John/Galivar had along with many others, left Europe for the new world, while others suspected that he was still alive and hiding in Yorkshire. However, that was where the story of the man behind the book mysteriously ended. The track had gone cold hundreds of years ago and it was unlikely that anyone could find the truth of the matter now.

His book was sent as a gift to the Bishop of Amiens, another occultist churchman who had had it copied several times and then hidden. Originally, there were reputed to be six copies and one original. The original remained where the Bishop had hidden it; no one knew where, but the six copies had been shared with a group of now famous occultists/alchemists by the good Bishop, who was an accomplished alchemist himself. The story, for there was a story about the book as well as about the writer, was that each of these six men had ultimately met with grisly and horrific ends and in each instance, the book was said to have been consumed by fire and thus returned to the Hell from which it had been spawned.

Edward also knew that much of the story about Devils, hellish deaths, and so on, was more than likely made up to scare anyone who might try to discover the truth. In the late 15th Century and even until modern times, there was a strong abhorrence of anything devilish or occult among most folk. Among some occultists however, there was a radically different version of events. Galivar was, in this version of events, thought to have been a true initiate whose work with elemental magic had afforded him some amazing powers. It was said that he could bring rain at will and walk through that rain without ever becoming wet. It was also said that he had discovered the invocation of elemental creation. Plainly however, something had gone seriously wrong in Bruges during the working of the ritual, but other than that, Galivar was in no way in league with any Devil. He was, in fact, almost certainly working for the other side!

The book was thought to hold the very ritual that Galivar had been attempting that night. It was said that whoever could unlock its secrets stood on the threshold of control over all Elemental forces and spirits.

Edward ran his fingers over the ancient leather cover of that very book. The fine leather felt smooth and soft to the touch. Was this the original or one of the six copies? Either way, just how had it ended up in a secondhand bookstore in London? The answers to these questions might never be known and to some extent, Edward didn't really care to know. It was enough that he held one of these seven books in his hands and had the time and luxury to study it.

The book itself comprised of seven chapters or 'books' and

each had of them five subsections. Edward instinctively understood that these five sections represented the four elements of Fire, Water, Air and Earth and the fifth was the fifth element or quintessence. The seven chapters probably had some relationship to the seven planets – Sun, Moon, Jupiter, Saturn, Mars, Venus, and Mercury and also to the seven metals – Gold, Silver, Tin, Lead, Iron, Copper, and Mercury. The number seven was a very mystical number echoed in the Bible, in mystical and magical texts, and even in ordinary life in the days of the week, for example. If this was truly the structure of the book then he already had an idea of how to start to interpret or decode it. The fact that the myth behind the book also spoke of one original and six copies reinforced Edward's confidence in this theory. This was, after all, an allusion to the hexagram with its outer six points and its hidden central seventh point. It was also an allusion to The Pleiades, a group of seven stars long associated with magic. Six of the stars are visible to the naked eye and the seventh is hidden. In addition, the seven could also refer to the seven major energy centers or chakras.

Of course, Edward was also familiar with the tales of misfortune and woe that had supposedly fallen on others who, like him, had attempted to decipher the Grimoire of El Natlez. He smiled to himself as he recalled one or two of the stories. He understood them to be allegorical tales designed to dissuade the amateur from seeking out the book at all. Almost certainly, there was little truth to the tales. Besides which, the key to avoiding a similar fate, according to the legends, was to have the wisdom to decode the book. Edward felt pretty confident that he knew how to approach this. After all he and Bainbridge, indeed, the entire lodge, had been preparing for this day for quite some time.

He opened the book once more paying very close attention to the opening figure of a seven-headed hydra that was emblazoned across the first two pages. His work had begun.

Chapter 9 – Going Home

William opened his eyes and immediately felt the coldness and uncomfortable stiffness of his body. He lifted his head, wiping away the sand grains that had stuck to his cheek. The ember fire was as cold as he was despite the blanket draped over him. He wiped sleep and grit from his eyes. The Sun had risen, but he was in the shadow thrown by a tall sandstone turret that jutted out of the desert like a sharp fang. He shivered.

"Good morning," said the voice from the night before.

William swung around to face the direction from which the sound had come. The man sat a few feet away on the same rock and was apparently still in the same position as he had the night before. He was dressed in jeans and a black poncho, his face hidden under his wide brimmed hat that was pulled down low.

"What happened?" asked William as he recalled starting to tell his story the night before and then nothing more.

"You fell asleep," said the man.

William didn't believe him. How could he have fallen asleep like that?

"Don't worry," said the man. "It was easier for me to have you sleep and to see your story than to listen to you tell it."

"See my story"

The man tilted his hat with one finger, pushing it up on his brow and for the first time, William caught a glimpse of his face. It was tanned or weathered or both. The bright blue eyes stood out incongruously in the midst of that face which on one side seemed to sag or be withered, as if badly burned and scarred.

"Yes. It was easier for me to simply view your experiences on the Akasha where it is recorded in all its inglorious details for anyone with eyes to see," he said.

William was silent as he thought about the several layers of meaning in the sentence Galivar had just spoken.

"Oh yes, William. You found me. Or… rather, I found you."

At that moment, almost as if on cue, the sunlight cleared the top of the sandstone turret and searing bright sunlight lit up the scene. Galivar smiled broadly.

"As you already discovered, I am living more or less a solitary existence out here in the desert with just the Eagles, Rattlesnakes, and Ants for company. Contemplation in such a place is, well, remarkably easy I feel," said Galivar examining the landscape around him. "Truly magnificent country and so close to the other worlds."

William shifted himself to a more comfortable position. He still felt quite stiff and despite the newfound warmth from the sun, he was very cold.

"I can help you. Yes, I will help you," said Galivar.

William felt a release of tension. He also felt certain inner warmth. It felt as if it shimmered around him and had a life of its own. It wasn't the warmth of the sun, but rather the warmth of spirit.

"Things never change," said Galivar. "Rather than understand how to gain the things you want through your own self, you seek, or rather, you fall into the trap of deception."

William blushed. He knew that Galivar knew what he had done. He was deeply ashamed.

"William, what is done is done my friend. Now is the time to undo it and to make amends. As the Christ said, it is time to repent. Now here is what you must do. You will walk back to your infernal pollution machine," he said, staring in the direction of the rented Ford. "You will drive back to Phoenix and from there you will return to London. You will carry on as normal for a few days, avoiding all contact as possible with the people you met that night. They will of course, become suspicious at your lack of contact, particularly given the commitment that you made and the 'gift' that they bestowed upon you. Within one week, your opportunity to redeem your soul will arrive and at that point William, you are on your own, for you must make the choice."

William was confused. "But, you said you would…"

Galivar interrupted. "And indeed, I will. When the time is right. I will. Not for you William, but for all of humanity."

William did not feel encouraged. The choice was his? Hadn't he already proven himself weak and ready to make the wrong choice? He needed help and he had sought out this man, this eternal living man, to obtain that help.

"William! Have faith in yourself. When the time comes, act and act willfully. Now, leave."

As Galivar spoke these words it was if he became transparent, shimmered for a while and then he was gone. He simply disappeared and he did so despite Williams despondent gaze.

"Leave," said a disembodied voice.

William stood. He was too weary to argue and he was resigned to his fate that he himself had sealed. His limbs still ached, but as he started to walk, they began to feel better and as he took one step and then the next, his mind wandered back to that night. He felt it. He sensed it. It was behind him. The dark thing was trailing him and he knew that there was not a thing he could do to escape. Maybe it already knew where he was and what he was about?

Chapter 10 – The Beast Within

Edwards' eyes were growing heavy. The poor lighting in his apartment didn't help, but then neither did the last 10 hours straight of examination of and meditation on the contents of Galivar's strange book. He stretched one leg and then the other under the table and immediately sensed cramp beginning painfully in his left leg. He got up and started to limp around his home office fighting the onset of the tightening of his calf muscle. He needed a short break, but he was determined to continue his examination of the book for several hours yet.

Stepping onto the balcony, Edward was welcomed by the warm air of an English summer's evening. The sun was setting and had already disappeared behind the two high-rise buildings in the distance, casting a long and looming shadow over Edward and his neighbors. He stretched with arms over his head and stifled a yawn before sitting in the chair he had strategically placed on the balcony for meditation. It looked quite uncomfortable having a tall straight back and a simple wooden seat. He closed his eyes and settled into a more comfortable position.

A face peered back at him. It was partly hidden in the shadows, but its' mouth was opening and closing as if it were talking soundlessly. Yes, he could now see the face better and it did seem to be speaking, but still no sounds emerged. Edward relaxed himself a little more and waited for the image to grow in detail and clarity, as he knew that it would.

"Who are you?" Edward asked in his mind.

The face seemed to look up as if aware of Edward for the first time. The mouth stopped moving and the lips became pursed.

"Who are you?" repeated Edward patiently.

The face began to change. The eyes deepened and grew wider while the nose took on more of an angular shape and the nostrils flared slightly. The mouth was thin and wide and Edward could feel a presence that he had been unaware of until that moment. He had felt that presence before though, but where?

"How dare you," exclaimed the face contorting as if raging against some unseen force. "How dare you!"

Edward involuntarily jumped at the sudden change in the demeanor of the face and the venomous spitting of its words had surprised him. He struggled not to open his eyes and break his meditative trance, as he knew that if he did, he would lose the opportunity to understand what was occurring.

"Who are you?" he repeated.

The face had now grown to such an extent that it filled his entire inner vision. It was no longer just a face, but was now a bloated black cloud of swirling dust particles with two reddened dots where the eyes had been.

"Edward Bright I warn you now to leave that book alone," shrieked the voice.

At this point, Edward had decided to protect himself and was mentally building a bluish-white light all around him, circulating this protective light and energy slowly around his body. As he wrapped this light around him it seemed to begin to have an effect as the shadow looked to be fighting against an unseen wind that was blowing and pushing it away from Edward.

"Leave the book alone Edward or burn in Hell," snarled the voice as the shadow appeared to be sucked up and away from Edward, finally disappearing with an audible cracking sound.

Edward again fought the temptation to open his eyes, but rather focused on a proper closing and protective ritual uttered in his mind, before stamping his foot on the floor and returning to normal consciousness. Only then did he slowly open his eyes. His heart was beating faster and he felt quite sticky with sweat from the involuntary sense of fear that he began to work on immediately. It was not good to fear an entity as it gave that entity a source of energy and, like a vampire after the blood from a willing victim, it would be back for more unless he could suppress it and regain control.

Control was key. Bringing his mind and imagination back under control would calm his body too. He took several deep breaths and uttered as he did so several lines of a text he knew that always helped calm him and helped him to restore control. It took him several minutes to do this, but eventually, satisfied that all was normal, he stood up and went to the kitchen where he would drink some water and eat a snack to further ground himself.

But what was the entity and why did he have a glimmer of recognition?

Edward sat munching on his salad replaying every aspect of his inner vision trying to place the sense of déjà vu that he felt. That some entity was aware of his attempts to read and decipher the book were no great surprise and he had taken many precautions already to avoid any trouble but again, why did he feel as if he already knew this entity? Why?

After finishing his snack, Edward returned to his study of the book. He would be there for several hours yet, whatever any entity said. In fact, the very fact that something, some entity had warned him off of reading and deciphering the book made him more resolute in his will to go on with the task at hand. Edward might even work all night now.

Chapter 11 – The Promise

William observed the woman closely. He knew that he was staring rather blatantly, but he couldn't quite help himself as she was by far the most beautiful creature he had ever set his eyes upon. Her delicate face delightfully framed by long, flowing, jet-black hair, and those oval-shaped green-blue eyes echoed his idea of womanly perfection. He quickly looked away as his stare accidentally and momentarily met those piercing eyes and his heart skipped a beat.

He picked up his coffee and took a sip of the hot bitter liquid returning his gaze reluctantly to the woman sat opposite. She was waiting for someone and he just knew it would be her partner. Someone like her simply had to be taken already – it would be just his luck if that were the case.

"You can have her if you want," said the voice.

William shivered involuntarily and tried to ignore the voice. It had been growing in intensity along with strange images and snatches of what he thought were conversations about topics he did not understand. Was he going mad?

"Excuse me, would you happen to have a light?" a soft voice interrupted.

His heart missed another beat as he looked up and into those clear azure eyes that looked back down at him expectantly. A slim cigarette was being held in his direction. She really was beautiful.

"I am sorry, I don't smoke," he heard himself say, regretting the fact that he had indeed quit a few years ago.

"Ok, thanks," she said moving on to another table in search of a light.

"It's in your pocket," said that voice.

William reached into his pocket automatically as if it were his own thought and was surprised to find a lighter there.

"Excuse me," he said, "I do appear to have a lighter after all."

The woman smiled and came back to lean into William giving him a glimpse of her shapely breasts and a whiff of the most divine perfume as she did so.

"Thank you," she said blowing out smoke. "May I join you?"

"Of course, of course," he said, a little too breathlessly, quickly clearing space at his table.

She pulled up a chair and shot him a brilliant white smile. "I appear to have been stood up," she said with a fake grimace.

"Stood up?" said William. "Who would stand you up? Well, that's good for me" he thought to himself.

"Oh someone," she said cryptically still smiling, her tongue protruding slightly from between those perfect teeth.

"She is yours," said the voice in his head.

Williams' smile faded slowly as he realized that that voice in his head wasn't his.

"Are you OK?" she asked, seeing his change of demeanor.

"Yes, yes, I'm fine, really, I just realized that I am supposed to be elsewhere and I'm about to miss an appointment myself," he said, regretting the words almost immediately.

"Oh, stood up twice in a row then," she said looking slightly piqued and taking a long and slow draw on the cigarette.

"I'm so sorry," he stammered. "I simply have to leave."

"Would you like my number?" she smiled and crossed her legs suggestively.

"Yes, er, fine, I would and maybe I can call you later?"

"I'd like that."

William stood up, stuffing his pockets with the papers and materials he was working with on the table, he dropped several coins on the table and hurriedly took the offered number scribbled on the receipt along with a heart sign, and made his way for the door. It was all a bit rushed, a bit panicked, but he was scared. That voice in his head - what the hell was it? He turned back and gave a half-hearted wave to the beauty that even now smiled at him, oozing good sex and good times. She waved back and mouthed, "Call me," making the sign of a phone with her cigarette hand as she did so. He nodded and escaped onto the street.

William had no idea where he was going or why. He just needed to run from that voice, but how to escape from a voice in your head? On the other hand, he was half inclined to go back and get more formally introduced to the girl, whoever she was, except that he dared not. It was a temptation, but it was a temptation he dared not give in to. Somehow, he felt that if he gave in, whatever it was that had entered his life that night would win and take over. He couldn't allow that and he had to fight, even though he did not really understand what it was he was fighting, or what was actually at stake.

Rushing down the street, William caught a glimpse of himself in the window of a store and recoiled in shock. He stopped and turned full on to gaze at the reflection. He was pale and it looked like him – dirty blond hair pushed back over his forehead, deep set brown eyes, a small moustache and thin pale lips but.... there was something odd about his appearance. Was it the haunted expression on his face? Was it something about his eyes that looked deeper set and darker than usual or was he imagining it all? He shuddered involuntarily and started walking again pushing through the shoppers and tourists on the London Street.

"You can't run," said the voice, followed by a sinister chuckle.

But William did run or rather hurry down the street. After another 100 yards or so he decided that he really must collect his thoughts and calm himself down. It made no sense to panic. A whiskey would help and looking around him, he spotted a small pub and made for the entry.

"A double scotch please," he said.

The whiskey tasted good and he almost immediately felt the heat surging through his veins as the alcohol entered his bloodstream. He slumped against the bar and signaled for a repeat double to the barman who was watching a boxing match on an old TV stationed above the bar. It had been four days since his meeting in the desert in Arizona, "four days" he thought to himself. So far, there was no evidence of any help from the man he had met there. Worse still, he was now hearing and acting on a voice in his head that wasn't his. He was hearing conversations and noises that didn't belong to him or his environment. Was he going mad?

He took the double scotch and sat on a barstool. He sipped the whiskey, this time savoring its fiery taste on his tongue before swallowing. He needed to think. Getting drunk wasn't an option.

He recalled leaving the desert in the car and making his way back to Phoenix where he had booked into a small hotel close by the airport and purchased a ticket for the flight out to London the following day. The flight had been non-eventful and on arrival in London, he had retired to his city flat to await something – an instruction, a sign, whatever it was going to be. Throughout that time, he had felt that darkness; a gloom even, like a heavy wet mist of despair descending over him and it had continued to grow in intensity. The voices and conversations had started sometime in that period too.

He cast his mind back several days more to the night of the party. The offer. He had thought it was a joke at the time. "Anything you want or desire is yours," he was told. The man who said it had huge charisma and an attractiveness that was almost magnetic.

William had been sat alone at his table awaiting Sharon's return from the ladies' room where she had gone to 'powder her nose'. It was Sharon who had taken him to the event with the promise of some hobnobbing with the rich and famous and, at first, it seemed as if that promise would be delivered on, as there were several movie stars and famous entertainers there. As he sat, William nervously became aware that he was being clinically examined from across the room. The man doing the examining smiled in his direction and came over to introduce himself.

"Ralph, Ralph Meister," he said, offering his extended hand.

William stood up rather nervously. He hated formality, but took the hand, flinching at the tightness of the grip offered back.

"William Dean," he replied.

"You look a tad uncomfortable William if I may say so old

chap," said Ralph.

"Well, yes, I do feel a little out of place and my friend has been gone quite a long time," said William.

"Might I sit?" asked Ralph.

Ralph pulled out the chair opposite and carefully seated himself. He placed both hands on the table in front of him and clasped them together before peering into William's eyes.

"You belong here just as much as anyone else William." He said. In fact, there is nothing particularly special about any of these people."

William was already partly mesmerized by this man. He looked as if he was in his mid-fifties but could be much older as there was elegance, even an aristocratic regalness about him. His hands were well manicured, his face deeply tanned, but lacking wrinkles of any significance, every dark brown hair was in place and the grey at his temples only afforded him an even more refined look. His clothes looked hand-made and they fit him perfectly.

"No, William. Everyone here was once just like you. A little shy, but with a curiosity of what life might be like under better circumstances. Most of them also had a sense that they ought to, deserved to be someone too, but in reality, they are no better than you or I."

Ralph looked around as if guiding William to do the same. William followed Ralph's gaze taking in the famous actress who leant against the wall arching her back in laughter as she joked with three men, a man he recognized as having once been a rock star who was followed around by two tanned and handsome younger men. It was like the who's who of fame and fortune in that room that evening.

"You see old chap? Just a bunch of people who got lucky."

"Lucky?" repeated William.

"Oh yes William, Lucky. They all got lucky when they met me," said Ralph his voice sharpening as he said the word 'me'.

William shot a look at Ralph thinking that he was joking, but Ralph gazed steadily into William's eyes and the intensity of the stare was enough to suppress any questioning. It was apparent to William that Ralph meant what he said.

"Ah, so you two have met then?" said a voice behind him. William spun around to see that Sharon had returned.

"Yes, indeed we have," said Ralph standing and making a small but very straight bow in Sharon's direction. "Excellent material my dear and William and I have much to talk about."

Sharon smiled. Evidently, she had other things to do anyway as she was dragged away laughing and giddy by another couple. "Listen to him William, you won't regret it," she laughed.

Ralph once again took his seat and took up the same position with his hands firmly clasped together in front of him.

"How would you like to be like these people William?" he asked.

"What?"

Ralph looked across the table calmly and repeated his question.

"Well, everyone would love to be rich and famous I guess," said William.

"Everyone? Or you would William?" asked Ralph.

"Why, I would of course, but come on, no one can promise something like that," said William.

Ralph smiled briefly. "Oh, I can," he said. He waited a few moments and then added, "I can and I will deliver too under the right certain circumstances."

There was a silence. Ralph continued to stare into William's eyes forcing him to look down at the table to avoid that penetrating gaze.

"How?" asked William, finally.

Ralph leaned back in his chair without taking his eyes off William's face. "Did he ever blink?" thought William to himself. There was a hint of a smile at the corners of his lips as he said, "That, my dear boy is the right question."

There was another pause as William waited, wondering if in fact, he was simply being played with, toyed with by this bizarre, but ultimately super confident man. He was curious however. He couldn't imagine how, but was it possible that a person like Ralph could give you a life of fame and fortune. And, if so, what would he require in return? William's thoughts were cut short as Ralph began to speak.

"What would you give William, to have it all? Money, possessions, beautiful women, sex, power? What would you give for that? What value do you place on such things? Ralph had leaned forward again drawing William involuntarily towards him. He could feel Ralph's breath on his face as he spoke. For a few moments Ralph stared into his eyes and this time William could not avert his gaze. Ralph's eyes were intense and there was nothing else in the universe except those eyes that glittered and shone and seemed to be like icy opals that stared past him and beyond into some other realm, some other universe where time did not exist. "Would you give your up your soul for such a life? Asked Ralph quietly.

"Soul?" repeated William. He felt strangely woozy as if drugged or tipsy, but this last question still seemed ridiculous. "Soul?" William's incredulity was bringing him back and he felt as if he was fighting sleep. He suddenly did feel extraordinarily tired, but he must not sleep. He must try to focus and stay awake. He must.

"Soul?" he murmured once more.

Ralph's eyes were growing more intense, but William was hanging on to the incredulity that he felt, trying to make that sense of ridiculousness his lifeline back to normality. "Mr. Meister, I cannot give you something that doesn't exist," he finally managed to say and with supreme effort, broke the gaze by looking down at the table again.

"Really?" said Ralph quietly after a moment or two of silence. "William, you certainly do have a soul, but perhaps you are not ready after all"

"Not ready?" said William reacting irritably and looking up. Again, those eyes caught Williams and he realized he had made a mistake. He began to feel drowsy again as the Ralph's eyes again drew him in and in.

"William, I am going to do you a favor. I am going to try a little experiment in order to convince you that I can give you these things and that you can offer me something in return of value." The softly spoken words washed over William soothing and relaxing him further. "I am going to give you a seed. The seed of all true power. If it takes root, then you will know where to find me. If it does not, then you will know with certainty that you have dismissed the opportunity of a lifetime."

William was now drifting as if afloat on a raft at sea, gently bobbing along. It seemed as if it rained a constant stream of warm water and the constant patter of the rainfall made him sleepier. Slowly bobbing along in the rain and the mist that obscured his view. He was cocooned in this place and he so wanted to sleep. A vague sense of something was stopping him from sleeping though and as he bobbed along on the raft he started to feel a greater sense of discomfort; even fear. In the mist, he imagined he could see eyes, many eyes, all just like Ralph's staring at him dispassionately. The mist was turning darker and the sound of the rain was like the beat of a drum rising and falling in intensity. Then he saw it. A shadowy figure that silently rushed up on him from out of that darkness in the mist and the feeling of terror he felt at that moment was unlike anything he had ever felt before. He wanted to scream, but it was already too late. William felt the shadow in his heart and in his mind. It had entered him and somehow, he could feel it cold and hard within him like a metallic foreign object.

William took another slug of his whiskey as he recalled the events of that evening. Even now he could feel whatever that shadow was within him. It called to him, spoke to him, and reminded him that it awaited his commitment – his soul. He knew that he simply couldn't last much longer and he hoped beyond hope that the man in the desert really would come to his aid and soon.

"Another," said William, holding out his empty glass to the barman.

William recalled how he had awoken the next morning in his own bed wondering how he had got there and shivering with horror as he remembered what seemed to have been a very bad dream. It had only taken a few minutes for him to realize that it had not been a dream as he felt the sharp metallic cold hardness that seemed lodged inside of him. He had immediately called Sharon who seemed to be expecting his call.

"Sharon, what the hell happened last night?" he had demanded.

She had arrived at his flat a half hour later.

"William, accept it and come with me," she advised. "We will go now to Ralph. He will explain everything and shortly, your life will change beyond belief. You will become one of the chosen few. Seriously, this is the opportunity of your life William. Why do you fight it?"

"You have done this then?" he asked.

"William, I gave him you and if you don't give in, my life is also in danger so please, please come with me, now" she said pleading with him.

"You gave him me?" he asked incredulously.

"William, I had no choice and you will see. It's a part of the bargain. Please William, come with me now."

William pushed Sharon away. He was confused. Betrayed and confused. "Get out. Get out now and leave me alone."

He took the glass from the barman and knocked the contents back in one gulp, anger flaring inside of him as he recalled that conversation. "How could she?"

"But you don't understand William, you have to come with me" she sobbed. "You have no idea how powerful IT is."

"IT?" said William. "What It?"

Sharon's face paled. "Ralph I meant how powerful Ralph is. You have no idea. Oh God, you have no idea at all."

"Look I have no idea what is going on here, but the last person I am going to see right now is Ralph. That man has done something to my mind," said William. "He also seems to scare the hell out of you so who is he Sharon? What have you gotten me into?"

Sharon shook her head slowly from side to side. She looked frightened. Very frightened. "I can't tell you William, but if you came with me you would find out for yourself and if you don't come with me then… God help me." Her words trailed off as if she was imagining exactly what would happen to her.

William had considered going at that moment. The look of fear on Sharon's face made it clear to him that, for her, it was truly important that he went with her. He even felt a strange sort of longing or yearning to go. He couldn't explain the feeling, but he knew it was not coming from him.

"No Sharon," he said finally and gently. "I am sorry, but no."

"Then you need to run and find some help William, before it is too late for you. It is already too late for me William, far too late, "she had begun to sob quietly. "There is only one hope. You must seek out the man they once called Galivar. He supposedly lives in the Arizona desert near Ajo on the border with Mexico, I think. He may agree to help you and he may be the only person who truly can."

Sharon began to back away from William, tears silently running down her pale cheeks. "Galivar. Find Galivar. He started all of this and only he can end it."

Sharon turned and almost ran from his flat leaving the door open behind her. He had not seen nor heard from her since.

The metallic thing inside him had seemed to wince at the mental mention of that name – Galivar. "But who the hell was he and how would he find him out in the Arizona desert?" he asked himself. He would walk a while and think. It was as he passed a sleazy looking internet café that the idea entered his head. "Why not do an online search? There can't be that many Galivar's!" he thought. Sitting at a PC, he typed in the name – GALIVAR and hit return. Several references came up. Several looked obviously incorrect yet one held promise and he hit the link. The website that came up talked of a long, lost book called the Grimoire El Natlez and a magician by the name of Galivar now long dead. His hopes were dashed. A dead man couldn't help him. He continued to read

57

though somewhat incredulously. Galivar was thought to have immortality and still be living somewhere the site said.

Under normal circumstances, William would have laughed this information off as a hoax or a fantasy. However, there was something about that metallic presence and its behavior that made him think there may be something to this story. The metallic presence seemed to be trying to stop him from reading. He was determined to investigate further. He googled Galivar and the name of the book again. It came up with several occult websites each of which seemed to contain exactly the same material as if all copied from one single source. They all said that Galivar had the secret of eternal life and even now was out working for humanity.

Again, his initial reaction was to laugh out loud. Rubbish! No one had eternal life, did they? His thoughts had switched to Ralph. How old was he? He wondered. The more he thought on it the more he began to think that maybe, just maybe there was something here to chase and hold onto. In fact, this was the only lead he had. He had to pursue it or he might just go stark raving mad.

William's next port of call was a travel agent. He booked his trip to Arizona right there and then.

Chapter 12 – The Lodge Meets

The smell of roasted chicken permeated the entire room and Edwards stomach rumbled as a direct result of the amazing aroma.

"Smells delicious," said Bainbridge with a smile.

Edward nodded his bird-like head and took another sip of his water. "I am famished," he said.

"Have you made any progress at all Edward?" Bainbridge asked peering across the table.

Edward delayed his response as McMaster entered the room bearing a large silver plate and the chicken. He placed it on the table and began carving the bird's succulent breast with a large and ornate carving knife. Both Bainbridge and Edward looked on expectantly and then began to help themselves to slices of chicken breast, dollops of garlic-mashed potato, and the assorted vegetables topped with gravy.

"Gosh, do I miss McMaster's cuisine," said Edward ruefully as he ticked into a forkful of chicken. "Delicious."

McMaster acknowledged the compliment with a small bow by the door and left them alone to their dinner.

"Well, our theory regarding the hexagram and seven being the key seems more than likely to be correct, but it is still quite tough translating the Latin and trying to interpret it, but yes, I do think I am making some progress," said Edward in between mouthfuls.

"Well, we are all rather looking forward to learning a bit more after dinner Edward. I do hope you came prepared?" said Bainbridge, raising his fleshy hand in Edward's direction.

Edward smiled over his plate. "Of course, I did and I am hoping perhaps the Lodge members can suggest some other angles or approaches to the task at hand. Although the key seems to work effectively, the translation is quite hard going and there are almost certainly a number of occult blinds designed to mislead one," said Edward.

Bainbridge nodded and swallowed. "Almost certainly."

"Who is coming for the meeting anyway?" asked Edward looking up.

Bainbridge pushed away his empty plate and leaned backwards allowing his belly to protrude more than it normally might over his trousers. He wiped his mouth with a white napkin in a grandiose gesture of satisfaction and belched more or less silently before answering. Edward smiled at this gesture. It was one that he had come to know quite well over the years.

"Not too many dear chap. Sedgwick for his expertise in Latin. Ex-Catholic priests do come in handy from time to time, don't they? Also, Davis who has studied the hexagram quite deeply as you know, Anna is also coming," he laughed a little. "How can I keep the young lady away," he said smiling at Edward's obvious embarrassment. "Also, I believe Frank Gall and his wife Joslyn will attend because of their work and interest in physical magic. That's more or less it I believe." He scratched his head and shifted in his seat loosening his belt a notch. "Got room for some treacle pudding? He asked.

Edward nodded as he emptied his mouth. "Excellent and yes, Treacle pudding… you spoil me."

"Not I Edward, not I. McMaster is very pleased to see you and it was he who suggested that he would prepare your favorite."

"If only I could afford him, I would prise McMaster away from you, I would," Edward said with a broad smile.

"Over my dead body young man," laughed Bainbridge.

Edward leaned back in comfort. He had spent many an evening in this ornate dining room discussing topics as far ranging as teleportation, mermaids, pagan Gods and Goddesses to the latest exploits of the English cricket team; a particular fascination of Bainbridge's not really shared by Edward. A crystal chandelier hung over the center of the polished oak table, but its light was too dim to truly light up the paneled room and so a number of other ornate lamps were placed strategically around the periphery of the room. Each of the four walls was covered in paintings of Bainbridge's ancestors and relatives who were somehow remotely related to Austro-Hungarian royalty, or so Bainbridge had always claimed. The effect was surely of a turn of the century dining room, but also it was homely, lived in, used, unlike many ornate dining rooms Edward had recently spent time in.

McMaster had prepared a double helping of treacle pudding for Edward allowing himself a half smile as he ladled custard over it, as he knew Edward liked. Edward sat back watching in appreciation and expectation.

"Thank you, McMaster. That looks truly delicious," he said finally.

Only moments after finishing the sticky and sweet delicacy in front of him, there was a sharp rap at the door and McMaster entered with Sedgwick in tow. Edward had never really liked or indeed, felt comfortable with Sedgwick, but Bainbridge trusted him. Sedgwick was a pale, hairy, and grossly overweight individual, who rather reminded Edward of a wild boar.

"Good evening," said Sedgwick. "I trust I am not too early?"

"Too late more like," said Bainbridge with a twinkle in his eye. "Too late for the treacle pudding."

Sedgwick smiled a faint smile that looked insincere and pulled up a chair at the table where Bainbridge had indicated. Sedgwick's obesity meant that even the slightest exertion caused him to sweat profusely and so as he sat there, he dabbed himself with his handkerchief. Edward was in fact revolted by the man; a defrocked Roman Catholic priest that Edward suspected was not entirely telling the truth when he blamed his occult interests for his priestly demise. Edward swallowed his distaste out of respect to Bainbridge and nodded hello over the table to Sedgwick.

Within minutes, all of the other guests had also arrived and were now seated around the magnificent oak dining table. McMaster had brought coffee and biscuits, and placed them in the center of the table. Edward had prepared for the meeting and, anticipating the attendees, he pulled from his leather briefcase a number of folders; each neatly identified with a name and passed them out to the assembled group.

"In your folder, you will find a copy of the main part of the manuscript along with my attempts so far to decipher it. As you will shortly see, the key of seven is plainly yielding good results, but in places, I am unable to decipher the Latin and, in others, I do not understand the result of the decoding. I have taken the liberty of highlighting various items where I think that each of you will be able to assist me with, though by no means am I limiting your assistance just to those highlighted areas." Edward stopped for a moment to take a sip of his coffee. "What we appear to have here is a ritual. It is a ritual that is designed to bring about some form of manifestation of the elements in my opinion. I am not certain as to what form this manifestation may take nor even why one would wish to perform such magic as yet, however I remain convinced that this ought to be something that we can establish or at least, make an educated guess at."

Edward looked around the table. The dim lighting cast many shadows and made it somewhat difficult to read Edward's small and neat handwriting. Sedgwick was reaching for his reading glasses while the others were maneuvering to find more light.

"Well Edward, I think you have done remarkably well so far," said the young woman opposite him.

"Thank you, Anna, but unfortunately a lot still remains to be done and I don't suppose that the manuscript will yet yield its true purpose very easily," said Edward blushing slightly under Anna's constant and admiring gaze.

"Interesting," murmured Sedgwick. He had developed large damp patches under his armpits that had formed darkened areas on his formal shirt that were emphasized by the lighting. Edward was repulsed. "Am I reading this right? To me, it appears as if an actual elemental spirit is invoked during this ritual," asked Sedgwick.

"Indeed. Although the name of the entity is in some sort of code I suspect and I have not yet identified the specific spirit to which it actually refers," replied Edward in a low voice. "Any ideas Frank?"

Frank, a frail gray haired man of indeterminate age, stirred as if to speak, but was interrupted by his wife, Joslyn, before he had a chance to say anything. "I don't think Frank has had sufficient time to make any determination in the matter yet, have you Frank?" asked the woman. Frank shook his head and pushed his glasses further up onto the bridge of his nose.

"I would urge utmost caution," interrupted Bainbridge. "If what we have here is a ritual that is deeply encoded and, if it truly does invoke a spirit of the elements that we cannot identify, we must be very careful even sounding out the words of the ritual in our heads." He warned with a frown.

Edward nodded. "I agree, especially given what we know about other attempts to decipher this book and, knowing that, if this is the ritual that Galivar was engaged in at the time of his 'accident', it may well be extremely dangerous or even seriously flawed."

There was a low murmur of agreement around the room.

"Looking at this Edward, I can tell you that this is no ordinary spirit," said Sedgewick as he studied the documents intently. "In fact, I would suggest that this is not so much an elemental per se meaning a sylph or salamander or similar, but something else entirely."

"What makes you think so?" queried Bainbridge.

"Its' name is an anagram for sure, but that anagram appears to contain more than just its name. It seems to also hold its rank," replied Sedgewick with a grim smile on his large face.

"And," said Bainbridge, somewhat impatiently.

"Well, it may take me a little more time, but I would say we were dealing here with the arch angel or possibly even, arch demon, with power over the elements or a specific element."

There was silence around the room. It was finally broken by Edward "What makes you think that?"

"One possible permutation of the anagram appears to be 'Lord of the Elements' or 'Elementals'," said Sedgwick grinning.

"The Lord of the Elements," whispered Edward almost to himself. "Where have I heard that name before?"

"You have?" asked Bainbridge. "I have never come across that name. Anyone else?" Bainbridge peered round the table.

Everyone shook his or her heads.

"Well, that's a good start Sedgwick," beamed Bainbridge. "Perhaps we can all examine the contents of this book over the next few days and then get back together again here to compare notes?"

Again, everyone nodded their agreement as McMaster entered the room with the drinks trolley.

"Anyone?" ask Bainbridge.

Everyone took a drink from McMaster and the atmosphere transitioned from serious and scholarly to more of that of a dinner party. Frank Gall and his wife made an early exit to no one's surprise as Mrs. Gall seemed to view her husband as very frail; needing frequent rest and little excitement. Sedgwick sipped whiskey quietly in the corner already studying the package carefully, while Anna used the opportunity to move closer around the table towards Edward. Steven Davis was engaged in deep and animated conversation with Bainbridge over two glasses of fine port.

Anna was quite an attractive girl with a shapely figure. She wore her hair simply; straight and long and was constantly pushing it back over her ears where it stayed in place for milliseconds before cascading forwards again. Edward guessed her to be about his age. He didn't find her unattractive. It was just he really had no time to be bothered with women. However, Anna had a redeeming factor at least and shared some of his interests.

"How are you Edward?" she asked, flicking her hair behind her ear on one side.

Edward smiled. "Fine, just fine. You?"

Anna smiled back. "Good."

It was a game that they played really, thought Edward. Anna was interested and always made it obvious. Edward was disinterested and made it also obvious. Anna would try to engage Edward in flirtatious conversation, flutter her eyelashes and flick her long hair, and Edward would totally ignore it, instead maintaining the conversation on a relatively formal basis. Anna would eventually give up and then a fine conversation would take place during which Edward would perhaps begin to think that he might just like her after all. However, no one ever invited the other out and so the game was played just the same each time ad infinitum.

"It is exciting to finally find the book?" said Anna.

"It really is. I have often wondered if it was just another story, or if the books were all in the hands of private investors gathering dust in some dark recess of a home library somewhere, but to actually have it in my hands… well!" replied Edward his face flushed with excitement as he spoke.

"I'm not too sure that I can help in any aspect of the research though," said Anna obviously seeking a rebuttal from Edward.

Edward chose however, to ignore her remark. His own comment had him thinking, remembering. "What was it," he thought to himself. It was there somewhere in his mind but he couldn't place it and it was annoying him terribly.

"Well, do let me know if there is something specific I can do to…."

"Pringle!" shouted Edward in triumph, cutting Anna off in mid-sentence. "Sorry Anna, but I have just remembered something that might be important. Something from my college days. I think that I need to go and visit an old professor of mine."

Anna smiled a sad sort of smile. The game was over for that evening anyway, but she also realized there would never be more than just the game between them.

Chapter 13 – Betrayal

Dr. Ambrose Pringle sat alone in the bar. He looked just the same as Edward had remembered him. Disheveled in a way that only a professor can be and at the same time quite peculiar looking. As Edward approached, Pringle's face wrinkled into a broad smile of recognition and he stood to greet him.

"Edward, my dear boy, how are you?"

"I'm fine thank you and doing very well thanks to the excellent education I was given. How are you?" said Edward smiling broadly.

"Oh, I am just the same." Said Pringle casting his eyes downwards.

"We haven't seen you at the lodge in almost a year, is something wrong?" asked Edward seating himself opposite Pringle.

"Oh no, just busy. Too busy. You know how it is," said Pringle pushing his glasses back up his non-existent nose. "But what can I do for you? How is Bainbridge? How are things?"

Edward brought Dr. Pringle up to date on all aspects of his life, the bank, the lodge, and Bainbridge over a glass of whiskey, while Dr. Pringle smiled and sipped his beer. Edward though suspected something was amiss as Dr. Pringle was not quite his usual cocky self, but seemed just a little out of sorts. He also looked a bit paler than usual.

"How about you?" asked Edward hoping to hear a bit more detail.

"Oh, just fine and very busy," repeated Pringle.

There was a short silence.

"Well, to be honest Dr. Pringle, I actually wanted to ask you something."

Pringle nodded and pushed his glasses up expectantly.

"Do you recall when Tony and I were late for your meeting arriving wet with a borrowed brolly?" asked Edward.

Pringle nodded.

"You told us a story about two men and a Lodge in Grosvenor Street – the ones that spoke to you telepathically?" said Edward.

Pringle nodded, but now seemed to be even greyer than before.

"I wanted to ask you if you could tell me anything else about that experience," asked Edward.

Pringle opened his mouth as if to speak and then stopped himself. He looked around in a manner that suggested he was trying to be discreet and then leaned across the table towards Edward.

"It's a bit awkward Edward to be honest," he said again peering from side-to-side and pushing his glasses yet again. "I'd like to tell you more but, well, I shouldn't."

He looked down again as if embarrassed. Edward was puzzled. He had never seen Pringle behave as coyly as this before. Usually, he was expansive to the point of being a bit of a show off and he adored being the center of attention, in fact, he usually set out to attract attention.

"Why? What has happened?" Edward asked.

"You know old chap, I really am not at liberty to say right now," replied Pringle more abruptly.

Edward took a sip of his drink. Something was amiss here.

"Another beer Dr. Pringle?" he asked. Perhaps if he could get Pringle more relaxed, a little tipsy?

"A half would be good," said Pringle smiling.

Edward signaled to the barman for another round.

"Well, I have some news for you," said Edward as the barman arrived with the drinks. "We have found it finally." He said with a look of triumph.

Pringle looked momentarily confused and then his face slowly changed, as he understood what Edward had said. "You found it? Excellent. But why didn't you tell me sooner old boy?"

Edward's strategy seemed to have paid off. In mentioning finding the book, Pringle's interest was piqued and now if Edward could get him talking and drinking, he might relax sufficiently to tell Edward what was going on. Edward brought Pringle up to date on the salient points regarding the discovery of the Liber El Natlez. He added scant details on their progress in deciphering it, as he didn't really want to give anything away. Something about Dr. Pringle's demeanor and behavior that evening had raised suspicions in Edward's mind. Pringle hung on every word though and was deeply interested in the news. So much so that he was promising to attend the next meeting of the Lodge and even offering assistance in helping to decipher its contents.

"Imagine, it exists and we finally have a copy," said Edward taking a sip of the whiskey.

Pringle seemed to be thinking as his eyes looked far over Edward's right shoulder.

"You know," he said presently, "that book is worth a fortune. There must be other groups who would pay a princely sum to have access to it."

Edward had him. "Hmmmm, I wonder how much it is worth and who would want such a book?"

"I happen to know a group that would pay handsomely for it," said Pringle who immediately looked nervous and checked around the bar one more time.

"Who would that be?" asked Edward.

"Oh, er, well just some people I bumped into recently. No one important and no one you would know."

"Come on Dr. Pringle. This must be a rather special group of people even to know of such a book never mind one that is prepared to pay a substantial amount of money to acquire it."

"Damn it!" said Pringle eventually. "Look, Edward, I can't tell you much, but the question you asked me…" Pringle looked grayer.

"Yes," said Edward.

"Well," he paused and looked confused.

"Was he going to share this information or not" wondered Edward as he waited.

"Ok. After that meeting when I told you my story, I decided I was going to go and find that book store again," he began at last. "Of course, it was no longer there. Long gone, in fact, and replaced by some fashion boutique, but the owners of that store recalled the bookstore and they managed to point me in the direction of someone who had been a regular browser of books there. I found him quite easily and I asked him if he knew of any Lodge in the Grosvenor Square area."

Pringle sat back and again checked around him and then continued with his story. "Not only did he know of such a Lodge, but he knew some of its members as luck would have it. I was intrigued. I asked for an introduction and eventually, I was introduced to the Grand Master of the Lodge at a party. He apparently didn't consider me a suitable candidate and I didn't see or learn anything about the nature of the Lodge or their ability to transmit thoughts."

"I see. But I don't understand why you couldn't tell me this earlier," said Edward.

"Well, and here is the thing. Since then, I have this crazy idea that I am being watched. Spied on. I can't quite explain it. It's a very uncomfortable feeling to be honest."

"But the book? What is the connection to the book?"

Pringle looked momentarily scared and again quite gray. "Well, believe it or not, the Grand Master asked me about it. He told me if I was to hear about a copy being found that I should let him know and they would be prepared to pay a considerable sum for it."

Edward now understood all he needed to know. Pringle had broken his Lodge vows. He had discussed his membership of the Lodge to this Grand Master. It was the only explanation.

"What did you tell him, this Grand Master?" he asked in a serious tone.

Pringle flushed. "Not much, but I wanted to establish my credentials and build his trust."

Pringle broke the ensuing silence "That's why I haven't been to the Lodge recently Edward."

"I understand."

Edward thought about this development. "Tell me more. Who is this Grand Master anyway?"

"His name is Ralph Meister. He seems to be well connected and very influential. The Lodge is, well, I wasn't sure how real it was because it seems to be a Lodge for the rich and famous from what I could gather. That's why I didn't fit. No money, no influence, and not much potential. My guess is that it isn't operating on our side either," said Pringle appearing relieved not to be admonished.

"No, I assume not." Said Edward thoughtfully.

"I didn't tell him very much Edward. To be honest, he seemed to know anyway about our existence and obviously, the search for the book as well."

"Yes," replied Edward. "That much is obvious, but how?" he said, more to himself than to Pringle.

Pringle now looked quite crestfallen and Edward thought he looked much older and paler. He felt a twinge of regret for putting Pringle on the spot, but his thoughts quickly focused on the man called Ralph Meister. What was his interest in the book and the Lodge? It couldn't be good Edward decided.

Pringle sipped at his half in silence. From time to time he looked furtively around and Edward suddenly realized what it was about Pringle. He looked like a hunted animal.

"Are you OK Dr. Pringle?" he asked.

Pringle looked surprised by the break in the silence as if the words had broken his thoughts. He pushed back his glasses and took a last long swig of his beer. Pulling his shoulders back he replied, "Edward, old chap, I am fine, just fine. Thank you. But I must go."

Pringle collected himself and his belongings, and held out a damp palm to shake Edward's hand. Edward took it and tightened his grip in an act of reassurance. They stood for a short while looking into each other's eyes and shaking hands. Then Pringle abruptly turned and made his way towards the door. He didn't look back.

Edward sat back down. He had to think. He needed to know

more about Mr. Meister and his lodge.

Chapter 14 – Astral Threat

William couldn't quite figure out where he was. Everything appeared indistinct; having an almost dreamlike quality. He certainly didn't recognize this strange place and he could feel his heart beginning to beat faster as his discomfort grew. Something really wasn't right. Not right at all.

He looked around physically slowly turning an entire 360 degrees. It appeared that he was in a hall of some sort. It was a very long and tall hallway, and very dark. He could just make out the walls in the distance and a doorway; huge double doors of carved wood. They were the sort of doors that go from floor to a high ceiling and usually would be expected to grace a room with very high ornate ceilings and chandeliers. Yes, it was some sort of hall; a grandiose hall or ballroom. But how had he got there?

"William," said a voice behind him.

He swung around instantly recognizing the voice. It had a husky, almost hypnotic quality to it and it belonged to Ralph Meister.

"William," Ralph's face leered a smile and he chuckled softly.

William found himself starting to back away, but somehow, he found that he could not. His legs seemed suddenly leaden and the floor sticky. He looked down to check if his feet were, in fact, sticking.

"William, you came as bidden. Well done," Ralph chuckled again. "Although if the truth be told, you really had no choice."

William looked up and into Ralph's face. It was indistinct too and it seemed to waver and wobble as if seen through a heat haze. He was instinctively drawn to Ralph's eyes and he felt himself succumbing almost immediately to their hypnotic gaze.

"That's right, chuckled Ralph. "Come in deeper William. Deeper and relax."

William fought to avert his gaze and managed briefly to look away, but then strangely, he felt his head turning to face Ralph. He cast his eyes downwards and realized in a detached sort of way that Ralph actually seemed to be floating. He had no feet. The recognition of this fact helped William to regain some concentration and he was determined not to look Ralph in the eye again.

Ralph chuckled and the chuckle echoed and reverberated around the hall space that they were in, growing in intensity. The whole place seemed to be vibrating along with the laughter.

"William," commanded Ralph as the laughter ceased.

William somehow managed to resist the urge to look up.

"Oh help, help me," William found himself saying under his breath as the fear rose. Where was he? How had he got here?

He repeated his appeal for help over and over again through clenched teeth with his eyes closed. He would not look at Ralph and he would not open his eyes. He was though drawn to do so as if some unseen and potent force were at work upon his subconscious. Slowly his head rose and he knew that, should he open his eyes, he would be looking directly into the face of Meister. He just had to open his eyes. He wanted to. He yearned to. He heard another chuckle, but it seemed to emanate from behind him. It broke his trance and he swung around, relieved to have an interruption. However, his relief did not last long. For there not three feet behind him was at first what looked like a cloud of dark smoke? As he peered into the dark, chuckling smoke, he realized that it had two unblinking coal orange eyes that stared back at him.

"William, meet your seed," said Meister's voice. "Meet the greatest gift that any man ever bestowed upon another."

William was horrified as he watched the shadow gradually take shape. He didn't want to watch. He didn't want to meet this 'seed'. He had a feeling of deep horror as the demon began to take shape in front of him. At least 8 feet tall, the figure seemed to oscillate in and out, phasing almost from something to nothing and back again. It was though, what he would have imagined a demon to look like. Humanoid but dark. Leering orange eyes. A snout and pointed ears that seemed human but then did not. Two small and blackened horns protruded from its forehead.

"William, this spirit can and will provide of its entire skills to help you with whatever you so desire. Power, money, sex, fame….. Anything that you want, it can provide to you. This powerful spirit can be your lifelong partner and guardian. It will watch over you, protect you, advance your interests, bring others under your control and even help you get rid of people you don't want around. It is power, William."

William only half heard Meister's words, although they seemed to echo deep within his psyche nonetheless.

"William…. Come on William, "Meister was saying. "You know how badly you have strived in life to succeed. You know how much you deserve this your reward? Be kind to yourself and accept this gift. It is, after all, what you have always wanted. It is the very reason why you attended out little party the other evening."

William knew that Meister was quite right. He wanted to be someone very badly and he had let little stand in the way of achieving his ambitions. He knew too that Ralph knew his flaws, his weakness, and his desires. He knew that whatever this thing before him was, it also knew.

"William, all you have to do is give in to those desires. There is nothing wrong with having a little bit of what you truly want and what everyone else strives for now is there?

William's mind was flooding with images of varying types. Nakedness and bodies interspersed with places and things. The demon was flooding his mind with everything that William had yearned for all of his life. The metallic heaviness was becoming a warmth inside that pulsated a sort of power and an attitude.

"But what do I give in return?" screamed William, feeling as if his will was slowly slipping away.

"Your soul." Said Meister. "Your eternal soul. In the afterlife, you will serve Him, your seed, in and through eternity. But, William. You don't believe in any life after death, do you? You have said many times that 'you only live once, so make the most of it while you have it'. So, what would you really be losing?"

William seemed to be surrounded by naked females who were pressing their bodies against him. They were writhing in ecstasy as they slithered around him, their naked flesh warm against his. He could feel the level of his interest as well. He was beginning to waver. This WAS his weakness and they knew it. "No," he screamed, closing his eyes again only to continue to see images in his mind.

"Enjoy it William. There is only one life, so use it well. Your words….", oozed Meister.

William could feel the women clawing at him, caressing him, kissing him and he knew that he could not hold out much longer. This was what he wanted. What he craved. He was slowly succumbing. He wanted to say Yes so badly.

"Meister," said another voice to the side of him quietly. William opened his eyes. He couldn't help it. He opened his eyes despite his not wanting to and he even managed to turn his head in the direction of the voice. He couldn't believe what he saw, but there to his side, surrounded by a glowing and bright light, stood Galivar. "How in the hell?" he thought to himself.

The women were gone. There was just him, the 'thing', and Meister. The thing was closer to him now, much closer. He could feel the heat of its foul breath upon his cheek.

"Meister," said Galivar again.

Meister looked shocked too. His composure lost and then regained all in an instant.

"Meister, I am here to tell you that you are playing with fire and that this fire burns. SEE," he screamed out the last word and once again the word vibrated the entire building as Galivar turned his face to reveal a badly scarred side to his face. "It burns Ralph and it will consume your very soul. It will consume your soul through eternity and unlike William here, you do know that you have a soul and you do know that you have lost it. You have clung to your earthly existence all of these years because you are afraid to transition into the hell that awaits you."

As he talked, Galivar seemed to grow in stature becoming bigger and more ... solid.

"Solid?" thought William. "How could that be?"

Ralph began to smile. "Galivar, how nice of you to pay us a visit," he said and began drifting closer towards the growing presence of Galivar. "I don't intend on burning in any fire. Not now, not ever."

Ralph raised a hand and pointed it towards Galivar. A faint greenish light tipped his finger and then flashed a stream of green light towards the figure of Galivar, where it surrounded him. Galivar simply shrugged and began to emit a very bright electric blue light that settled like an aura all around him, pushing the green light outwards and eventually the greenish color disappeared altogether.

"Not a very pleasant welcome Ralph, for an old friend" said Galivar.

The blue light aura began to rapidly expand throughout the room and as it passed over William, he felt a surge of energy pass through him. As the light reached Ralph and the thing, they suddenly disappeared. One second they were there, and then suddenly, gone. William looked to Galivar for an explanation, but everything was now a deep electric blue color and fading away into nothingness.

William opened his eyes and lay still. He took in a sudden deep breath, let it out again and sat bolt upright. He was in his own bedroom. He was utterly confused. Was it a dream he had just experienced then? His heart was beating rapidly and he could still feel a sense of fear. It must have been a dream.

"Hello William," said Galivar's voice.

For the second time that night, William jumped and swung his head around in the direction of the voice. Even in the darkness, William could see the outline of Galivar standing by the door of his room. Galivar looked ghostly, like a bluish colored transparent wraith.

"William, you must pack and leave. Look for a man called Edward Bright here in London. I will lead him to you. Now, I must go but the time for your decision is near."

The figure dissolved and William was left wondering if he had awoken in another dream so he pinched himself quite hard and then flinched in pain. It had been a dream, but a living, lucid dream. The voice inside his head was laughing. It was getting stronger that voice that he now understood to belong to that thing; that demonic entity that would want eternal servitude in return for a few years of wanton sex, money, and fame. He tried to ignore it, but it was very difficult. It was as if there were two voices in his head now. One, he recognized as his own and the other. The thing. He shivered.

He got up and washed his face in cold water staring at himself in the bathroom mirror. His own face stared back. "That was reassuring," he thought. What now? Who was Edward Bright and what did he have to do with this?

He had so many questions and yet, he had not a single answer.

Chapter 15 – Meister

Edward now knew he had to find this Ralph Meister, but first, he had to find out who he was and more importantly, what he might be. Edward knew that he had to be careful. He would need to cautious and deliberate, as any error might well prove to be fatal. He briefly consulted with Bainbridge by phone. The two talked for a few minutes as Edward brought Bainbridge up to speed with the situation. Bainbridge would instruct members of the lodge to put out feelers; both physical and astral feelers, to see what could be discovered. He urged Edward to be careful. Edward agreed not to act rashly and would await further information back from Bainbridge.

Edward decided that one approach might be to meditate. To make contact with his higher self to seek guidance and insight, so he retired to his temple. His temple was in fact the spare bedroom that was marked with the four quarters and contained a small cupboard that when opened, served as an altar and contained candles and other items. He opened the cupboard and lit the candles, watching as the flames stabilized and the wax around the wick melted slightly. He then retreated into the center of the room where he performed a cleansing ritual and then sat cross-legged on the wooden floor.

He closed his eyes and cleared his mind. The trick was to think of nothing, but to watch whatever pictures emerged in his mind. He would follow the pictures, which he knew from experience would become animated and start to move like T.V. images. After a short while, the pictures would become more like a movie being played out inside his head. A movie that he could fully participate in and even direct a bit if needed.

As he sat silently, he focused on his breathing and its regular rhythm. In and out, in and out. He then began to imagine that he was breathing not only with his lungs, but with his entire body in that rhythm, in and out, in and out. He was like a sponge breathing in air and breathing it out of every pore in his body. The rhythmic breathing began to have an effect and he started to drift inside the darkness of his mind. After a short while, the darkness took on a bluish hue and half-baked images seemed to form.

At this point, the trick was not to react to the images, nor to think any thoughts. The mind needed to be silent. He was a silent watcher observing the images arise and fall in his mind. He did not react to any of the images. He did not judge them, but rather, made sure that his mind remained completely silent.

An image of a face arose and transformed itself into a building and then he seemed to move backwards away from the building so that the building became one of many in a long street of such buildings. His field of view broadened and broadened and at that point he spoke two words in his mind. Ralph Meister. The image froze momentarily and then refocused as he began to pick up speed moving over the rooftops at incredible speed until one building came rapidly into view. He sailed towards the building slowing as he did so and entered a window to step inside a room.

The room contained a large, heavy oak desk and chair. There was an ornate fireplace and above it on the chimneybreast, an oil painting of a fearsome demonic figure. He had to work hard to control his mind at that point, for the image had made him recoil a bit, and he began to lose the images. He focused and stopped the thoughts from arising. He stopped the question that he had been about to give word to in his mind and the image brightened up and became clearer again.

Behind the desk was a man. He was working on a computer, but looked up disturbed. The door opened and another male figure entered the room and sat on the edge of the desk. The two of them seemed to be talking animatedly. But what were they discussing? Edward couldn't hear anything. He could only see the images. After a short while, the second man got up and left the first man alone again. He sat staring into space for a moment and then, turned and stared right back at Edward.

The eyes dominated this man's face and those eyes could see him. The man stood and began to walk towards Edward. The man uttered a few words and then it went completely black. Blackness filled Edward's inner vision. It was a pure menacing darkness. In that darkness, Edward began to sense a presence. There was something about the presence that seemed slightly familiar. The darkness seemed to coalesce slowly and began to take shape. It was as if a cloud was forming all around him. The cloud was heavy and cold. It seemed also to be a suffocating darkness as Edward was beginning to have an issue breathing regularly and began to feel tightness in his chest. A heaviness that was growing and growing and threatened to stop his breathing altogether. Edward had to act and act fast. He would need to exit his remote viewing session in an explosive way. This was dangerous, but he felt that he would be unable to confront the being that he now knew was forming in front of him. With every ounce of will power that he could still muster, he imagined himself releasing energy by exploding like a bomb and instantly, he was back in his temple room.

Edward now would need to spend some time rebalancing the forces in his body and spirit as the explosive method of return left one in a state of energy imbalance that was unhealthy. He started to undertake a set of inner rituals that would help restore that balance. He was sweating. He was burning he felt. He had too much Fire energy. The solution was water. He needed to drink water and fast.

Edward got up, feeling the weakness in his legs after sitting immobilized for so long. He reached out for the glass of water that he knew was just a few feet away and drank of it greedily. As he drank, he could feel some balance being restored in his body. He was cooling down. He would still need to spend some time with some ritual work however, in order to balance his psychic bodies too.

With his rituals over, Edward began to feel better. Two things had surprised him. Firstly, he was surprised at the fact that the man he knew to have been Meister had been able to see or sense his astral presence in the room and, secondly, that he was protected by such a powerful entity. What was the entity that had begun to form? There was something familiar about it and yet he had no recollection of ever experiencing anything quite so powerful. He needed to reassess the situation. He needed help and he needed to properly prepare to confront Meister. Meister plainly had protective help, but then so did Edward. He needed the Lodge to help him. That was the only way.

Chapter 16 – Find Edward

William thought that he had found Edward Bright. There were several Edward Bright's in the phonebook, but William thought he knew which of the Edward Bright's he was looking for. As he ran his finger down the list of names, addresses and phone numbers, the voice in his head had made a certain noise. It was a growl. Yes, the best way to describe it was as a growl. The growl had occurred as his finger passed by one of the Edward Bright's. That was his man. The voice in his head had given the game away, he thought.

He dialed the number, but there was no answer. He would lose no time doing what Galivar had suggested. He would pack a few items and leave. He would go to the address in the phone book listed for this Edward Bright. That was all he could do.

An hour later, he was stood opposite the address. Lights were on and someone was home. He crossed the road, opened the small metal gate and walked towards the solid wood door. He reached up to knock, but as he did so the door opened and a man stood there looking surprised.

"Edward Bright?"

"Yes," said the tall man filling the doorway. "What do you want? I am just on my way out. A matter of some urgency."

William knew exactly what to say.

"Galivar sent me."

The shock on the other mans' face was clearly visible. The man at the door took a deep intake of breath and peered more closely at William.

"Galivar?"

"Yes, Galivar."

There was a moment of hesitation and then the man dropped his shoulders as if in recognition that his plans would need to change.

"You had better come in then," said Edward, moving to one

side.

Inside, William could see Edward more clearly. Edward had recovered a bit and the look of shock that had crossed his face was now replaced with a look of interest.

"Come in, come in. You know Galivar?"

"Yes, I have met him." William replied.

Edward ushered him up a narrow staircase and into a sitting room.

"Take a seat."

William sat.

"Who are you and why are you here?" asked Edward, removing his overcoat and sitting down on the other chair in the room.

"My name is William, William Dean. I am here because I am in some trouble and Galivar told me to find you and that you would help me. It all seems a bit far-fetched I know, but it is the truth."

Edwards face remained impassive. If he thought it sounded far-fetched, he wasn't showing it.

"Yes. Galivar? How do you know Galivar?"

William began to explain. He told Edward about his meeting in the desert and then began to tell him about his meeting with Ralph Meister, but was interrupted.

"You know Ralph Meister too," said Edward, sounding surprised.

William told him about the meeting, the Lodge, the people he had seen there, the promise, the seed Meister had planted and the voice and presence in his head. Edward nodded his head slowly as he listened to the story. For Edward, things were becoming significantly clearer.

"You said Galivar had sent you to me. Why?" he asked.

William explained about how it had been for him over the past few days and about his experiences in the ornate room and how Galivar had intervened and then shown up in his flat telling him to find Edward.

Edward shook his head now. There was a look on Edward's

face that suggested that he was thinking many different thoughts but not really listening.

"First the book and now Galivar himself," said Edward almost to himself. He shook his head again. "Well, look, I don't know how you found me nor whether your story is the truth, but I do know one thing. You are not safe here." Edward stood up and put on his coat.

"Let's go. I will take you somewhere safer. There we can digest your story a bit and try to figure out what it all means. First, I need to make a quick call though. Please stay here until I get back"

William was surprised how quickly Edward returned. The tall, rather gaunt figure had a serious look on his face. "I have consulted with someone I deeply trust and we think the best place for you is our Lodge," Edward said. "Come on, let's go."

Chapter 17 – A Command

Meister sat at his desk. It was a large and sturdy, polished oak desk. Each leg was fashioned after the symbol for one of the elements that any devout Christian might recognize as the four holy living creatures. The origins of the desk were not well known but it had probably been crafted for someone with an interest in alchemy for it had a secret drawer that only opened by pressing a sequence of ornate characters carved around its edges. The characters represented the four elements and the seven planets or metals. Only someone with occult knowledge would know the correct sequence. The desk took up most of the space in the small circular room that served as the Grand Masters office at the Lodge. The room, though circular in design, was divided in to the four quarters again representing each element and in the South, was a large and ornate fireplace that had gone unused in quite some time.

Meister was reading. His small glasses sat on the end of his nose and from time to time he rubbed his neck involuntarily. The report was written in a small but legible hand and it was a briefing on another group of magicians in London led by a Grand Master that Meister knew was really nothing more than a neophyte. Cyril Bainbridge was the sort that Meister despised. An occultist through birth and privilege, rather than by hard work. However, the organization that he led had some potency and one should never under estimate the enemy. He had been tracking this Lodge for some time as it had been infiltrated by one of his own disciples. They had something he wanted. He wanted it badly. A book. He also suspected that one of the Lodge's members had been spying on him using remote viewing.

Meister pulled himself away from deciphering the small handwriting and reached over the desk for a small glass of whiskey. He took a small swallow and marveled at the heat of the liquid in his throat. Fire was his very favorite element, he thought and he had it in droves in his psyche. He was driven, focused, and intense. He consumed information as if it were fuel for his inner fire and his will was finely tuned like a laser. He had worked hard to achieve his powers and then he had had a very interesting encounter with the Being that he now served. While this Being held mastery over all of the elements, it too had a particular liking for fire.

    Meister sat back and recalled how many years ago, he had made contact with this Spirit and raised his contacted Lodge. The power that it provided was beyond virtually anything wielded by any politician or billionaire. He was the master of the world's destiny by virtue of this contact and he knew it. After all, most of those billionaires and politicians were already enslaved by their physical desires to the will of the Lord of the Elements along with innumerable others, for over that time, he had set up over 100 other sister Lodges around the world. A subordinate Grand Master that did his every bidding led each. The contact was his and his alone. Though each recruit also got their own demon to help them too.

    As he understood it, Galivar had been the original choice to manage and oversee the Lord of the Elements plans but at the last minute, Galivar had proven himself unworthy. Meister wondered about that. How could it be that the Lord of the Elements was mistaken? On the other hand, human nature being what it was, he could understand. The weakness was everywhere. The faith in something good, something eternal, had always shone in some quarters. The darkness knew that it could not extinguish it for if it did, it too would cease to exist. Instead, the darkness needed to hold the light at bay. Keep the light hidden in the corners and hiding in unusual places. Ralph allowed himself a small chuckle. The light was so naive and yet it too knew that it could not be eliminated completely and so it seemed content to find a place in the souls of the useless, the misplaced, the people who had no ambition, and no need for things or power. Meister let out an audible scowl. How he despised them and the light they held.

    A sharp crackling sound suddenly caught his attention and he realized that the master was about to appear before him. Meister stood stiffly in anticipation. The form that started to materialize was large and shadowlike and yet it was made of flame. The flame was of another fire however – the opposite of brightness, the opposite of Fire too in a way, and yet it was fiery. He bowed as the form became distinct and yet remained indistinct.

"The time has come," said a deep and far off voice in his head that boomed and reverberated around his mind. "Even now the final act in our play is being written. I do not expect you to fail Meister."

Meister nodded. He did not expect to fail. Failure was not possible. He held all the keys, had all of the knowledge and there was not a chance in hell of failure.

The figure began to fade away leaving a smell of sulfur and an excess of electricity in the air that cracked and pulsed around him for a short period until all was again calm.

Ralph returned to his desk and the report. Edward, now he was an interesting character, thought Meister, but Sedgwick had him well covered. Sedgwick reported that Edward was intelligent, knowledgeable, and yet soft. His innocence and gentleness were his weaknesses along with his naivety. However, it seemed that Edward and the Lodge he served were growing closer to understanding the book they had found. That would not do. Not at all. Ralph needed that book and he needed it before it was acted upon.

Ralph was a believer in coincidence. Many occultists are. So, when he picked up the phone, he was unmoved by the news.

"Grand Master," said Sedgwick. "I have important news. Edward has just arrived at their Lodge with our potential new recruit, William. If we strike now, we can obtain the Grimoire, William, and put an end to Bainbridge's plans to decipher the book."

A slow smile crossed Meister's darkened features. "Good. Very good, in fact. The Master will be pleased."

He could imagine Sedgwick's smile on the other end of the phone. He was such a sycophant, but he had his uses. He placed the phone back in its receiver and stood up. Action was required.

Chapter 18 – The First Battle of Grosvenor Street

It was quiet, peaceful, and dark on Grosvenor Street. The building that served as Bainbridge's Lodge was well lit however, and the occupants were engaged in an important early hours' discussion. Edward had two issues. Firstly, what to do with William and how to help him, and secondly, when to undertake the ritual outlined in the Grimoire. When he had arrived at the Lodge with William in tow, he had been given some very good news. It appeared that Frank Gall had made a breakthrough.

"You were correct about the number seven being a key, Edward," Gall had told him, William and Bainbridge. "The key is the hexagram which though commonly associated with the number six is actually representative of the number seven, but there is a sub-key. That sub-key is the three Alchemical Principals of Sulfur, Mercury and Salt that can be discerned and further understood by deeper study of the hexagram."

Edward immediately knew what Frank had discovered and he could hardly contain his excitement.

"Of course! He proclaimed.

William looked bemused. He and Edward had taken a cab to this building seeking refuge from Meister's Lodge. On arrival however, nobody had actually even noticed his presence because of this excitement about deciphering some book.

"Six pointed star. The symbol of the Elements. With the Fire triangle overlaid by the Water triangle resulting in the symbols for Air and Earth within the same symbol. It fits with Sedgwick's thoughts on the Lord of the Elements perfectly. The three Principles of Alchemy….. Yes, yes, perfect!"

Edward's mind was racing now even as he removed his coat and indicated for William to do the same.

"All becomes clear to me now Frank." He gushed.

Frank nodded and beamed a broad smile across his pasty-colored face. For a moment, he looked anything but frail.

"What other symbol would this Lord of the Elements utilize? He asked.

"Exactly," replied Edward.

By now, they had reached the Grand Master's office where Bainbridge awaited them with whiskey.

"A toast," said Bainbridge. "A toast to Frank and to the Lodge."

Everyone touched glasses. William was grateful for the whiskey, but a bit concerned that his situation appeared to have been completely forgotten.

"Ah yes," said Edward suddenly. "Everyone, this is William. We will come to his problem shortly as we have a new conundrum to solve."

Edward looked around the room smiling broadly. He was very pleased. He knew how to decipher the Grimoire and could now do so with relative ease. All he needed were a few hours of quiet in order to complete this task.

"Where is Sedgwick?" he asked.

"He is on his way," replied Bainbridge.

Edward knew that the Hexagram held many arcane secrets. Not only did it reveal the four Elements, but it also showed that the Above and the Below were mirror images of each other. The microcosm and macrocosm were reflections of one another. It was perfect symmetry and the perfect solution to boot. The hexagram contained the numbers three, four, and the six, and seven. Combining the three and the seven or the six and the four resulted also in ten. It was perfection. Now all that was required was to interpret what the opening narratives of the book meant by looking at the correspondences with the hexagram. It wasn't a trivial task but it wouldn't take him long either.

Edward's thoughts returned to William and the problems at hand.

"Well, how do we begin?" he asked, looking quizzically at William. He then began a long monologue explaining William's dilemma taking some time to reveal that William had been in touch with the book's author – Galivar. There was surprise around the room at this particular revelation. What a coincidence that Galivar, the mysterious adept who had written the Grimoire, had come into their world more or less at the same time as they had discovered how to decode his book.

Bainbridge poured more whiskey. Despite William's woes, there was almost a party atmosphere at the Lodge that night.

#########

Outside, three men sat in a car. Sedgwick was sweating profusely despite the chill in the early morning air. In truth, he felt bad. On the other hand, the metallic voice inside his head was gleeful and he took note of that and tried to be gleeful too. Carefully, Sedgwick, Meister, and Williams, got out of the car. The box-like object they had brought with them was quite fragile and it needed to be handled with vigilance and care. They crossed the road with equal care and entered the small yard of the Lodge building. The box was placed carefully on the ground outside the front door; a magnificent solid wooden door finished in glossy black paint. Meister removed the red silk cover to reveal a carved wooden box. However, this was no ordinary box. Inside, it contained a rolled piece of copper much like a piece of copper pipe. Inside of that was another metal. It was essentially a battery, but one with a very specific and sinister purpose.

The three men stood over the box for a short while. They joined hands and looked upwards arching their backs. Meister began to chant quietly, almost under his breath, some words. After a short while, the box containing its occult battery, began to emit a steady hum. As the humming sound increased, the chanting grew in volume and a faint greenish glow seemed to emanate from the box. Suddenly, Meister stopped his chanting and fell silent. After a minute or so, he broke hands with his colleagues.

"Shortly, we will enter," he stated simply.

#########

It was Frank that first noticed it. He wasn't much of a drinker and he had left his whiskey largely untouched after the initial toast. There was a strange smell; almost like rotting eggs or bad drains. He wrinkled his nose and then sniffed a couple more times. He was also beginning to feel quite warm. Not only that but the party-like atmosphere was evaporating as the air seemed to become slowly stagnant and heavy.

"Something is afoot," he said.

Edward nodded his head. "I had been expecting this," he said. "To the Temple."

Once inside the Temple, Edward made several hand gestures as he sealed the room. Bainbridge assisted him and then they all retreated to the center of the room. The Temple room was simple in design. The floor was paved with black and white tiles, and in each quarter, was a small square window that had been blackened to reduce the light that it let in. There was a simple table altar set with candles and on each wall a printed image of an archangel was hung. They sat on the floor in a circle facing each other.

"Let us all meditate on the Light," said Edward quietly.

There was silence in the room save for the rhythmic breathing of the small group of people now sat in a circle.

Suddenly, there was a banging sound. It was so loud as to make more or less all of the gathered company jump in unison. The sound reverberated around the Temple room, which had a high ceiling and was structured to amplify sound.

"Stay focused," said Edward calmly.

Another huge booming sound reverberated through the building and then silence again. The atmosphere was becoming denser and denser and it seemed to all in the room that it was getting very much hotter as well.

It was Edward that saw it first. His heart jumped a little for he already recognized what it was he was seeing. It wasn't good. In the corner of the Temple, a hint of smoke began to fill the room. The smoke grew in density and began to swirl rapidly around itself almost like a mini-tornado. He kept his eyes on it and soon, everyone else had become focused on the smoke activity in the corner. Slowly but surely, the smoke column began to take its shape. It was shaped like a large humanoid head with piercing red eyes.

"Don't look at it," said Edward as calmly as he was able.

William too recognized what he was seeing. He understood now that there was no escape for him tonight – not ever - and that he was inevitably doomed. If the Lord of the Elements could materialize so easily within this sealed and protected Temple, then there was not much anyone could do to stop it from growing within themselves was there?

The atmosphere became dull and metallic-like somehow. It was now getting cold as well, as if all the heat energy had been utilized by this demonic being in order to take form there. An oppressive and sinister atmosphere pervaded the building.

"William," said the booming voice that now reverberated around the Temple. "William, by now you know what it is that you yearn for and that with the seed within you, you are yet already one of us."

Beads of sweat rolled down William's brow despite the icy cold. Fear gripped the pit of his stomach and he looked to Edward seeking some sign that he should resist.

"Do not listen William," said Edward, noting the look.

Inside William's mind, another voice was talking. It was telling William how puny these people were and how weak they were. It was telling William how great he would be and how much influence he could command as a man of power."

"William, look at me," said Edward aware that something was extremely amiss. "Look only at me and into my eyes."

William tried. Indeed, he wanted to, but it was impossible.

Laughter erupted from the thing in the corner and now that laughter was reverberating around the Temple. Louder and louder it grew until, for William, it seemed to be become everything. The entirety of his reality was now laughter and he was echoing that laughter. He was being sucked into the sound and he could feel himself gradually slipping away. It was a terrifying but inevitable process of simply being sucked unconsciously away it seemed to him.

Edward stood. He began to utter certain words and phrases. He was shortly joined by Bainbridge who followed his lead. The words were quickly drowned out by the swirling, hysterical laughter and yet, the pair continued to chant in unison. In the corner however, the demonic humanoid being was still growing in both size and solidity.

Abruptly, William, who could stand it no longer, broke the circle and began to run headlong towards the smoke figure. All he could hear in his mind was the laughter and it was a sound that seemed to welcome him home finally. As he entered the smoke, he found himself apparently floating, as if cocooned, protected, and safe. Then he simply lost consciousness.

Edwards' face was now covered in small beads of sweat. He sensed that whatever the thing in the corner was, it was far more powerful than he was. It was like attacking an elephant with a fly swatter. His strength was slipping away and, as he glanced at Bainbridge, he could see how pale his face was and how old he suddenly looked. There was a last moment of despair before everything seemed to go black.

######

Edward seemed to be floating. All was dark and he was disoriented.

"Do you not remember me?" a voice said. It was a thunderous voice. "We have met already Edward," it said.

"Come now Edward, you must recall your friend's little Ouija party?"

Edward's mind instantly replayed the events of that evening long ago as a stream of pictures inside his mind. He remembered. He now remembered all the other times they had met too.

"Yes, re-awaken Edward. Re-awaken."

Chapter 19: A Decision is Made

Galivar watched the events at Grosvenor Street unfold within his mind's eye. As he had thought, the Lord of the Elements was simply too strong and too powerful to be stopped by a well-meaning, but not very advanced, group of magicians. If only, they had had more chance to study his Grimoire and perhaps even go through with the ritual that was documented there. Then, they would have had a half chance at least. Now, it was left to Galivar. Though in truth, he had always known it would be. After all, it was his mess. He would have to – was obligated even to - clean it up. It was the only way that he could finally move on.

He could see them even now. William, Edward, and the others. Each was locked in a small room blindfolded and loosely tied to beds. This was good, for it meant to Galivar that William had still not given up his personal struggle and perhaps also to indicate that Edward was also still considered a threat. Otherwise, William and Edward would both be untied.

Galivar had, in fact, been waiting for this moment for hundreds of years. He simply had to put things right. It was not only revenge for a dark deed done to him by a trusted colleague but a putting right of what he had inadvertently put wrong. The damage done to human souls over the last centuries was, in part, on him and although he had done his best to pay off some of that karmic debt, he still had to resolve the issue once and for all.

######

William shivered. He was icy cold. Inside, he felt utterly destroyed. He had little or no will left and the voices, his voices, inside his head were now totally dominated by the other more alien voice. His own mental voices seemed weak, indistinct, and unimportant by comparison. His will and his fight was leaving him.

"William."

"Wait though, whose voice was that?"

"William," said the voice again. It was clear, bold, and loud. He recognized it more or less at once then and the effect of hearing that particular voice was to immediately lighten the darkness, the melancholy, and the guilt that he felt.

"William, the choice remains yours," said Galivar's voice.

He could feel the other's attention now too. The other thing was now getting closer again as if to protect its now wounded and frightened prey. The darkness, the metallic hardness, was returning.

"William – choose and choose now," he heard Galivar say.

Choose? How could he choose? He had little or no will. He was tired and quite honestly, he didn't think he knew how to choose at all. The shadow seemed to rise up and to tower above him menacingly. He felt the chill of it deep within his being.

"Choose," said Galivar again.

William pondered in an abstract sort of way what a choice was and how such a choice might be made. It was a strange feeling he had as he thought through this for he felt as if he was now in another place and time altogether. Where he was, there was utter peace and calm, and yet he knew that the shadow hovered over him ready to devour his soul and extinguish any light that it may find there. But that was where his body was. He, whatever he was, was somewhere else. He was calm and he was safe there.

What is choice? He thought.

A stream of thoughts replied. Choice was the absence of choice. Choice was a choice that was not made for himself, but made for the higher being. He was an instrument of the action as opposed to the actor itself. Choices, real choices, were made at a higher level within the self and they reflected the true will.

He saw then something approaching him visibly in his mind.

She approached him slowly and purposefully from a distance. She was the most perfect female that he had ever seen. As he looked into her beautiful and radiant face, he felt as if she were the perfect partner for him – his soul mate. He felt that he had known her for all eternity or longer. He had dreamed of her all of his life.

She was the woman whose perfection knew no bounds and all other women were simply a poor copy. He knew also that she had always been there with him. He knew true love in that instant. She smiled. It was a gentle and patient smile.

"No," she laughed, her eyes wrinkling playfully. "I am not your soulmate William. I am your very soul."

He heard her words and he understood. If this is what he was giving up, then it was simply too much to ask. The woman smiled again. She came close and hugged him, drawing him close into her embrace and he felt as if he were home. This was heaven surely? Suddenly he felt strong and whole again.

"The choice has been made," said Galivar's voice in a commanding tone.

The shadow was gone in an instant. The metallic heaviness lifted. It was replaced by the faint smell of roses and the most magnificent weightlessness William had ever known. A massive burden had been lifted from him and he had been blessed with a gift. He had met and embraced his own higher self – his soul. He knew what he truly was. He knew true love and he understood what he had almost given away – almost lost forever. He had stood on the precipice of his own demise and for a few moments had been ready to leap. Now, he had stepped back from the precipice and he felt strong, purposeful, and resolute.

William struggled at his bonds with a renewed strength and energy. He soon discovered that he was not tied so well and was quickly free. He removed his blindfold and shut his eyes as they grew used to the light level in the room. He stood up and reached for the door. It opened easily and was not locked. In a matter of minutes, he had released Edward and the others, finding them also loosely tied and blindfolded in adjoining rooms. He felt bold, powerful, and certain. He also knew that Meister knew this. He was all too aware that of that.

They made their escape surprisingly easily. Too easily perhaps?

Chapter 20 – A Ritual Attempted

They regrouped at the Lodge. While Edward seemed deeply troubled, William was acting like a new man altogether. He urged Edward and the lodge members to prepare to conduct the ritual in the Grimoire immediately.

"We must do the ritual. That is what Galivar tells me," he said urgently.

Edward shook his bird-like head slowly. "We are not prepared, not ready. We haven't yet finished figuring the book out. We simply can't," he said heavily.

"We must," argued William. "We have no other choice."

Bainbridge looked old. He was more than aware of his frailty at that moment and sadly, even more so of his true lack of magical ability. He was also still in deep shock over Sedgwick's treachery. They had been friends for many years. "If Galivar wants us to do the ritual then the least he could do is join us?" he said.

There was a short silence as they all sat deep in thought. "Do we even still have the book?" said Edward suddenly. Glumly, Bainbridge confirmed that Meister now had the book. There was another extended silence.

"So," said William, finally breaking the silence. "We have lost the book and in doing so, we cannot perform the ritual without help from Galivar? You have your notes, though right?"

Edward nodded. "Yes, but I didn't make an entire copy. In retrospect, it should have been the first thing that we did…"

"So, where is Galivar and how do we get a hold of him?" Asked William. "Come on, you must have some idea?"

Edward smiled a grim smile. "Indeed. Now, please be quiet and let me try."

He closed his eyes and sat upright in his chair placing his hands on his knees. He began to breathe rhythmically and slowly.

Initially, he could see nothing. Nothing but the blackness

behind his eyelids. Then a bluish violet color appeared. It was a sign that Edward recognized as an indication that he was reaching the right state of consciousness. He called out in his mind to Galivar. However, although he became aware of another presence, he immediately knew that it was not Galivar. The presence was a more familiar one. There was a chuckle. Edward shuddered and attempted to keep his breathing calm. A face slowly appeared in his field of vision.

"I can teach you the ritual Edward," said the face. Edward felt himself hit by a wave of raw energy that unfolded inside his head like a packet of information. Within milliseconds, Edward knew the entire ritual – the words, the invocation, the positioning and type of candles, incense, everything. He snapped his eyes open.

"Edward?" asked Bainbridge.

"I have it."

#######

A number of hours later, Edward, William, Bainbridge, Frank, and the others were in the Temple and ready to commence the ritual. Everything had been carefully prepared. The ritual was not a group ritual, but rather a ritual for an individual and Edward would need to perform it alone. The others would simply observe and offer protection if necessary.

With a small nod, Edward signaled his intention to begin. He slowly approached the alter and lit two red candles. Stepping back, his words were just an inaudible murmur to his captivated onlookers. He dropped to his knees and held out his arms making a cross shape with his body. Then in a louder and clearer voice, he called upon the four elements using several references to each in turn. He called upon their archangels, the Holy Creatures, their magical properties, and named each in several languages. He then stood and moved to the south calling repeatedly on the Fire element to reveal itself for several minutes before falling silent again. Then, after a few minutes of silence and meditation, he lit the incense and another candle, before returning to calling upon the Fire element over and over again for several minutes.

Abruptly, he stood and lit a fire in a shallow but wide, gold-colored dish. The fire leapt up quickly and seemed to begin to take on a form of its own, like a curtain of flame. Within the curtain of flames, a face slowly began to appear. A face formed of flame and heat.

"Hail, The Lord of Fire," shouted Edward.

At this point, Edward was feeling a sense of euphoria. He had succeeded in the ritual evocation of the Fire element using Galivar's original ritual. He raised his head and stared at the flame face that protruded from the flame wall.

"Hail Natlez!" he cried.

When the fire elemental spoke, it seemed as if the entire Earth resonated with each vowel and consonant. Each syllable sounded like the thunderous emanation of a volcano erupting. The building shook.

"Hail Zeltan, it said.

#####

Several miles away, Meister felt the spoken word vibrations also. At that very moment, he had been smiling at a shared joke with Sedgwick about how inept Edward and his friends were. He had been laughing about their hurried escape, which he had watched with amusement from an upper window. He had been promised by his Master that these people would be dealt with directly by Him. Even now, he had assumed that the Master had already condemned their souls to hell. However, as the Earth vibrated in tune with the words of the Lord of the Elements, Meister felt something he had never expected to feel – ever. He felt his own age.

He felt it as a sudden and sharp intake of breath and he knew that this was also his last intake of air. As it whistled into his lungs, he watched in horror as the skin on his hands started to simply crumple with age and how skeletal he became. The Abbott of Bruges watched in the horror of a momentary eternity in which he knew with all certainty that, rather than being victorious this day, he had utterly failed. He recalled in full detail in those brief instants, how he interrupted his colleague's - Galivar's - work in the cellar that night and hijacked his magic and his ritual. He recalled how he had watched Galivar through time, observed his experiments, and attempts to work physical magic. How he had coveted that ability and power. How he had willfully stepped in with a few of his own monks who truly thought Satan himself was being summoned that night. It had been his moment of glory and the only failing of that night was that Galivar had somehow managed to escape and then eluded him over the centuries. That Galivar had even managed to record the ritual in his damned Grimoire and then have it copied and distributed was even worse. The entire time that Galivar and his book existed, there had always remained this threat to Meister.

As the face of his Master arose in his fading consciousness, he knew that he had never been the disciple his Master had planned for and now, apparently, the Master had swapped him with another. He was discarded, he was dead, and hell bound for eternity.

Sedgwick watched with horror as Meister seemed to simply disintegrate and implode in front of him, collapsing to the floor – a smoking heap of dust and bone. Sedgwick couldn't help throwing up.

####

Somewhere across London, Galivar also sensed the vibrations and he knew that the Abbot of Bruges, Ralph Meister, was now in hell where he fully belonged. There was no satisfaction in this knowledge though. It simply meant that someone else had managed the ritual in true accordance with the Law, whereas the Abbot of Bruges – Meister – had hijacked another's attempt – his own – and deserved this end for it.

Galivar could now finally move on. His mistake had been rectified and he knew or sensed that it had been Edward and William who had made this possible. He was wearying of eternity and tired of hiding in the shadows, Galivar was finally free to pass into the light. This was a decision only he could take and he was ready to take it. He had one last task to complete before he could do so however and he would do that shortly. Galivar allowed himself a small inner smile. Meister, the Abbot of Bruges, was now serving his Master for all of eternity.

####

Zeltan laughed and stretched himself as tall as he could. The body felt strange, but he had achieved his physical incarnation finally. This body, this Edward, was now the mirror image of Him. As above, so below. Natlez was the mirror image of Zeltan, but on a higher plane. He had escaped his limited existence in the spiritual realm and now had a physical presence as well. Most useful.

"He is dead," said William almost incredulously. "Meister is dead. The ritual has worked."

Bainbridge looked to Edward for confirmation.

"Yes, Meister has met his end," said Edward-Zeltan.

A collective sigh of relief emanated from the tense observers in the temple.

Edward's eyes glinted strangely. There was an unfamiliar look about him and Bainbridge was suddenly concerned.

"Edward, what is wrong?" he asked.

Edward was standing in such a way as if he were trying to add inches to his already commanding height. It was as if Edward was trying to grow beyond his physical body. He turned and looked coldly at Bainbridge.

"Edward? said Bainbridge again.

"It's not Edward," mumbled Frank. "It's not him."

William's newfound strength was fading as he too realized that Edward was, well, different somehow.

It was at that moment that Edward collapsed in a heap to the floor.

Chapter 21 – Zeltan Takes Command

The group carried Edward to a nearby room and laid him on a sofa. His face felt hot and he seemed to have a fever. Bainbridge had found some ice and laid a cold compress on his forehead to try to take away some of the heat. Surely this was a side effect of the ritual?

As Edward lay with his fever, the group slowly began to disband as each decided it was time to leave. Only William and Bainbridge remained behind. Bainbridge was worried about Edward whereas William was suspicious of what may have taken place. On the other hand, William no longer heard that other voice in his head, nor did he feel as if he were carrying a massive deadweight around with him. It seemed to William as if the ritual conducted by Edward had solved William's problem just as Galivar had suggested it would. He now wondered about his friend, Sharon, and hoped that she too was now free of the fear that she had obviously felt. He wondered also about all of the others he had seen that night at the party. What would happen to them?

William had learned something important through this entire experience though. He had learned that he was actually happy with his life exactly the way it was, or had been before he had met Meister. His life was genuine. His world was his own responsibility created by him consciously and unconsciously. He was suddenly full of gratitude for that life and its meaning, which no matter how irrelevant he was as a person, he was his own creation. It was a startling revelation for a man who had always sought confirmation from others and had always covertly, and sometimes more overtly, looked for fame and fortune. He was thankful now to Sharon and to Galivar for they had led him to and beyond this critical crossroads in his life. He was also thankful to Edward, for Edward had somehow managed to tune into Galivar and conduct the ritual that had mattered at the moment that it had mattered most.

More than that, William now understood more about who and what he was. He knew that he had a soul and that his soul was precious. He had learned something about polarity in that his soul was feminine and he now began to understand Man's yearning for the Goddess figure. He now believed in Elementals, magic, and demons. He understood something about how it all worked and what reality was. He knew that from this day forward, he would need to keep on seeking for answers and understanding and that his quest, far from being over, had just begun.

Edward began to come around and moaned slightly. Bainbridge confirmed that the fever was broken but encouraged Edward to remain resting on the sofa for a while. Pale and gaunt, Edward seemed to have aged dramatically in the last few hours and he looked exhausted. Edward nodded and closed his eyes.

"I think you should leave William. Edward will be fine and I will ensure that he recovers, "said Bainbridge.

William nodded. He too felt exhausted and needed to sleep. Furthermore, he suddenly realized how hungry he was. He needed to eat and then sleep.

"OK, I will come back though, as I would like to thank Edward for he saved me from a fate worse than death."

Bainbridge nodded and saw William to the door.

"It's been a long and exhausting day for all of us," he said as William stepped outside. "Take care and get some rest."

Bainbridge returned to Edward and found him trying to get up from the sofa. He was however, still dizzy and seemed unable to stand.

"Edward, rest. You have been through a lot," he said.

Edward nodded and slumped back on to the couch momentarily before sitting up again.

"What happened?" he asked.

"What happened?" replied Bainbridge. "You made the ritual. I was going to ask you the same thing. What happened? What was the face? Who is Zeltan?"

Edward's gaunt face looked blank. "I did?"

"You did. You have no recollection at all then?" asked Bainbridge somewhat incredulously.

"None," said Edward, laying back onto the sofa. "I am so dreadfully exhausted though."

"Yes, you need to rest, dear boy," said Bainbridge. "I shall stay with you."

In truth, Bainbridge was worried. Firstly, he wasn't sure what the ritual had actually achieved, he was nervous about the effect that it seemed to have had on Edward, and he was more than a little concerned about what may have become of Sedgwick? Was there still danger from the black lodge? He didn't know but he wasn't going to take a risk. He sat heavily in an armchair and tried not to doze off himself. He too was tired.

Bainbridge woke several times during the next several hours. Each time he shifted position in the armchair but always making sure to check on Edward. A number of times, it was Edward's voice that woke Bainbridge anyway. He seemed to be passing in and out of feverish nightmares and at least twice, Bainbridge got up to check his temperature and found him to be quite warm. Finally, Bainbridge stirred again. Dim light was now beginning to flood the room from windows as dawn broke. As he opened his eyes, Bainbridge's heart missed a beat when he saw that Edward was gone.

####

Zeltan had awoken in a strange place. A portly figure slumbered in an armchair nearby and Zeltan moved quietly and swiftly to avoid waking him up. He needed to discover where he was and why he was there. After a couple of false turns in the dark, he found himself in a hallway and soon found the front door. Once in the street, he looked for a cab but it seemed as if it was the early hours of the morning and all was pretty quiet. He strode purposefully down the street. He knew where he was going and what he needed to do but he was unclear as to how he had wound up in that strange room. His last memory had been of finishing the ritual. He smiled to himself as he walked. Few, if anyone else, could have undertaken that ritual successfully. It took an accomplished magician.

Zeltan now recognized where he was and saw a number of taxi cabs parked outside of a hotel. He hailed one, got in and snapped an address. It wasn't far but at this time of day, it paid to be careful. He paid the fare on arrival and set off towards the door of a building on the street. Strangely, he didn't seem to have any keys and had to resort to ringing the doorbell. A few moments later, Sedgewick peered around the door, his eyes showed shock and surprise.

"Well, don't gawp man – let me in!" barked Zeltan.

The door opened and Sedgwick stepped aside. Zeltan brushed passed and then turned.

"Sedgwick, where are my keys? I seem to have mislaid them? he said.

Sedgwick, looked puzzled and mopped his brow with his handkerchief. He opened his mouth as if to say something and then closed it again.

"Well?" said Zeltan again in no mood for fun and games.

"Well, er, Ed..." start Sedgwick.

"Look. I would like you to bring a new set of keys to my office immediately. I have work to do." Said Zeltan, turning and marching off down the corridor and up the staircase. He soon found his office and entered. There he could finally unwind and relax at his familiar Oak desk. There was a knock.

"Come," he shouted.

Sedgwick entered clutching a set of keys. He placed them on the desk but seemed hesitant.

"Yes?" asked Zeltan.

Sedgwick wrung his hands and glanced around the room nervously.

"Yes?" repeated Zeltan.

Sedgwick swallowed hard. "I'm sorry, who are you?" he finally asked in a small voice.

Zeltan chuckled. "Who am I?" he laughed. "Why, I am Zeltan, Sedgwick. I am Zeltan, I am the greatest magician that ever lived and I am here to change this reality for the Master. I am the Grand Master of this Lodge."

####

Bainbridge was worried. Where had Edward vanished to and why? He made several calls looking for Edward but no one had seen him. Then, out of the blue, Edward simply walked into to the Lodge and into the reading room where he sat and began work on his notes regarding the Grimoire.

"Edward?"

Edward swung around. He looked fine. His usual self.

"Ah Bainbridge, thought I'd spend a bit more time on my Grimoire notes. They need to be preserved now that we have lost the book to Meister's Lodge." He said.

Bainbridge nodded and sat in a nearby chair puzzled and concerned.

"Edward, are you feeling OK?" he finally asked.

"OK? I have never felt better, why do you ask? Replied Edward.

"Well, since you conducted that ritual, got a fever, and then simply vanished….."

"Oh, did I?", said Edward in a faraway voice that Bainbridge knew simply meant Edward was not really listening.

Suddenly, Edward swung around in his chair.

"You know, I think I finally figured out the ritual's intent." He said his eyes flashing. "We thought all along it was to conjure an elemental of some sort from which to learn about the Elements but I'm not sure that was truly the intent. No, I think Galivar intended something else. He intended to become one with that Elemental and truly bring it through to our reality."

Sedgwick nodded though he was fairly lost already. "Go on," he said.

"Well, it seems that Meister hijacked this ritual and took the place of Galivar and in the process used this power for his own ends. I think that what we did was to restore what should have been so that Meister met his demise while Galivar gained what he had always intended and has now moved on charged with the Elemental's power."

Edward spoke excitedly now. "William was the catalyst for all of this. Interesting huh?"

Bainbridge nodded. "Yes, interesting. I do hope William is alright.

"Oh yes, I'm sure he is," Edward beamed and went back to writing furiously in his small but neat handwriting.

"But what was it that we saw? The face in the fire?" asked Bainbridge.

Edward stopped writing and put the pencil tip in his mouth contemplating the question. "Why, it was the Lord of the Elements," he said. "I empowered him to get out from under Meister finally and restored him to Galivar. At least, I think that is what happened."

"You know Edward, this is all becoming a bit much for me. I realized yesterday that I am a pretty poor magician and I am getting rather old."

"No," said Edward, looking concerned "that is not true."

"Yes, Edward, I am. It is time to hand over this Lodge to you."

Edward considered this quietly for a few moments. "OK, if this is what you truly want, so be it. However, I will need you close at hand."

Bainbridge nodded slightly disappointed at Edwards willingness to comply.

Epilogue

William whistled a favorite song as he made himself boiled eggs and toast for breakfast. He felt happy and carefree for the first time in a very long time. Furthermore, the sun was shining and he planned to take his breakfast on his deck in that sunshine. There, he had a view of part of the city overlooking a park. As he neatly cut the top off of the boiled egg and placed it in the egg cup, he was rethinking over recent events. He wondered what had happened to Galivar? He also wondered about Edward and made a mental note to call him later in the morning to check on his wellbeing. There was so much about the past few days and weeks that was actually unbelievable. "After all," he thought, "How many people would believe in men that lived for forever and could wield immense powers or, groups of people in London organized into Lodges practicing magick?"

It was at that moment that he became aware of a presence behind him. Swinging around in his chair, he found Galivar standing there on his patio!

"Gosh, you need to stop doing that!" he said.

Galivar smiled ruefully. "Don't worry, you won't see me again after today. I have no further purpose here and I will transition myself into the light shortly. It is just that I have some unfinished business William and now I need your help."

William chewed his mouthful of egg and toast so that he could ask the inevitable "How so?"

Galivar moved toward him. William marveled at the fact that Galivar's form seemed complete and full. His body was in the room with him but also, it was somewhere else. He knew that Galivar was bilocating, or being in two places at once, something credited to many Saints and Magicians.

"Many years ago, I wanted to learn how to control the Elements. Back in those times, such an ability would have afforded me greater understanding of the physical world and its mysteries. In order to do this, I called up a great force – an elemental spirit with knowledge of mastery over the physical world. Its name is the Lord of the Elements.

"Yes," said William. "we have met."

"After years of work I was ready but, unknown to me, my friend and mentor, the Abbot had been watching my progress and he stole my ritual at a very critical moment. The result of this was that I have spent centuries hiding in the shadows while he, created a network of people to which he gifted great powers using forces he truly did not understand. You knew him as Meister. I watched his rise to power and saw how he took the corrupted powers wielded by The Lord of the Elements and put them to use – his own self-serving use. I also believed that it was my responsibility to put right what I had done in allowing the Abbott to usurp my ritual. That is why I preserved my ritual in the book know to you as the Grimoire of El Natlez. I knew that at some point, someone would conduct the ritual and put back what I and Meister had let out of Hell."

Galivar paused.

"Go on," said William.

"The problem is William that something is not right. Edward performed a ritual but not the one I outlined in the Grimoire. It was similar I believe but it was not mine."

William stopped chewing. He recalled the way Edward had behaved after the ritual and his subsequent fever.

"My time approaches William for I must move on but I am also wanting someone – you? – to investigate what happened a little further and to ensure that the situation does not get out of hand. Will you do that? For me?"

William had many questions but there was no question that he would do as he was asked. He had to as he now knew that something didn't add up and something was awry. He nodded his head as the body of Galivar began to shimmer and fade away.

William stood up leaving his half eaten boiled eggs and made a call. He needed to check Edward.

####

Other Books from Asteroth's Books

Asteroth's Books publishes books about ghosts, the paranormal, and other strange topics.... Here is a selection of other titles available.

Thomas Bauerle

Kanashibari: True Encounters with the Paranormal in Japan (Kindle, Paperback)

G. Michael Vasey

The Black Eyed Demons Are Coming (*Kindle*)
Ghosts of the Living (*Kindle*)
True Tales of Haunted Places (*Kindle*)
The Most Haunted Country in the World – The Czech Republic (*Kindle and paperback*)
The Black-Eyed Kids (*Kindle and audio*)
Your Haunted Lives – Revisited (*Kindle and Audio book*)
Ghosts In The Machines *(Kindle and audio book)*
How To Create Your Own Reality *(Paperback and Kindle)*
God's Pretenders – Incredible Tales of Magic and Alchemy *(Kindle and audio book)*
My Haunted Life – Extreme Edition *(Paperback, audiobook and Kindle)*
The Mystical Hexagram *(Paperback and Kindle)*

Sam White

Will We Meet Again? *(Kindle)*

http://www.asterothsbooks.com

Made in United States
North Haven, CT
23 November 2024